ALSO BY ROZ

The Only Easy Day
The Paramedic and the Writer
The Soldier's Tale
The Summer House
Three
Undercover Lovers
Valentine 2525
Worlds Collide

Totally Bound Publishing
Back Home
Moments
The Carpenter and the Actor
The Doctor and the Bad Boy
The Fireman and the Cop
The Teacher and the Soldier

Extasy Books
The Demon's Blood
The Guilty Werewolf
The Incubus Agenda
The New Wolf
The Third Kingdom
The Vampire Contract
The Warlock's Secret

Dreamspinner Press
For a Rainy Afternoon

MLR Press
Seth & Casey

NOTES & ROSES

STANFORD CREEK BOOK ONE

ROZENN SCOTT

NOTES & ROSES
THE STANFORD CREEK SERIES – BOOK ONE
Published worldwide by All Romance eBooks, LLC
Safety Harbor, FL 34695
AllRomanceeBooks.com

PUBLISHER'S NOTE
This is a work of fiction and any resemblance to persons, living or
dead, or business establishments, events, or locales is coincidental.

ISBN: 978-1-943576-84-5

First Printing, June 2016

DEDICATION

With grateful thanks to Rachel Maybury who helped me so much, and to Elin Gregory and Sue Brown who said so many nice things.

To everyone who supported me in my MF group, and had the faith I could write MF. ☺

To my proofers…Christina Manole, Hanne Lie, Rick Mulholland, Tyra Berger and Dawn Mayhew.

I love you all.

And, always, for my family.

CHAPTER ONE

Megan Campbell stepped away from the cash register of Notes & Roses and leaned against the back counter. She put her right hand in her jeans pocket and, as carefully and unobtrusively as possible, removed her cell phone and scrolled to Justin's name. What should she text her brother? *Help* sounded like a good start. Or possibly, *there's a man in my shop and I think he's drunk or stoned.*

Yep, text something like that to Justin, and he would come in guns blazing. Then he'd pin the weird guy to the floor and read him his rights. And the man currently staring at a wall didn't look dangerous, just lost. Homeless, maybe?

Something more specific then, like, *there is a vagrant in here, and he needs help, what should I do?* The man moved a little. Away from her side of the store, the "roses" part of the setup, and over to the "notes" side. He was peering at the shelves, a collection of stationery and household bits and pieces like cushions and local crafts. He stumbled a little, turned to the side, and looked up at the posters displayed on the far wall. Landscapes of Vermont:

rivers, small towns and red high-sided barns with gently rolling hills of emerald green.

"That's wrong," he said.

"Sorry?" Megan asked—but he didn't reply.

He's talking to the wall now. Should she add that to the text as well? This was going to end up being a hell of a lot of typing to explain what he was doing. Despite how odd it all looked, the visitor wasn't threatening her. Also, Rachel would be back soon. Maybe between them they could sort this out?

He hadn't even spoken to her, but something wasn't right. Maybe it was the way he'd been standing, his hands fisted at his sides, staring now at the new Valentine's wall display of flowers and hearts. Maybe it was the way he was dressed; dark jeans caked in mud, heavy boots that had tracked in the same mud. Not to mention the black hoodie with the hood partially hiding his face from her view.

Or maybe it was the despair in his hunched shoulders, the utter defeat in the way he had to support himself to stand.

Whatever it was, Megan was faced with two options. Talk to the strange man in her shop while she was alone in here, or call in reinforcements in case things went south.

Her visitor moved, not his feet but his fists, unclenching and bringing his hands up to knuckle his eyes and then cover them. Megan's cop brother liked to explain these things to her, but she didn't need his help to recognize when despair in someone turned to anger.

She sent the standard 911 text, startled when she looked up and saw the stranger had stepped closer to her while she'd been distracted.

"Where am I?" he asked, his voice very soft.

"You're in my shop."

He shook his head. "I need the music. Someone took it, and I need it."

Okay, this was so not going the way she wanted it to go. He was incoherent. Maybe he was homeless and needed a place to get out of the persistent snow that had plagued Stanford Creek the last few days. He'd evidently been somewhere slushy and muddy, if his clothes were anything to go by.

"I don't understand, sir; what music do you need?" she asked, and waited for him to acknowledge her question. Instead, he took another, shaky, step forward, and covered his eyes again. "Hello? Can I help you?" she repeated when he didn't look at her.

That finally got his attention. His hands came down, and she got her first clear look at his eyes and face. What she saw had her reaching to send another text. He had blood on him, smeared down from his temple into his wild beard, and his blue eyes were bright with something. Drugs maybe? Long, dark hair hid some of his features, and he looked like he was about to keel over.

"Where's the music?" he mumbled, his voice low and urgent. He gripped his temples hard and stumbled back, knocking a display of greeting cards to the floor. The sound was a loud clatter in the otherwise quiet room. "Shit... I didn't..."

"Sir?" This time she was within reaching distance as he rounded on her, his lips pulled back in a snarl— or a grimace of pain, she couldn't be entirely sure. Whatever, it wasn't the look of someone who wanted to be spoken to. *Time to leave.* She glanced at the front door, imagining the steps between here and there and whether or not he would lurch her way. When she focused back on him, all she saw was a situation that could get out of hand. He was a good six inches taller than her five-nine, broad and built, with tattoos curling around his wrist, disappearing up under the sleeve of the hoodie.

Everything about him looked wrong. He didn't move again, or even acknowledge her; all he did was stare with bright sapphire eyes, focused on a point behind her, scary and intense and so damned fixated with his expression in that scowl.

"What happened?" He groaned and covered his eyes again. "Call... Zee..."

She texted without looking, only glancing at the screen briefly to make sure she was sending another text to her brother and not some random person on her list. *911. Again.* The standard sibling instruction for *help me right the hell now*, reserved for having one of her brothers rescue her from one of her many dreadful first dates. Garrett wasn't even in town, so there was little point texting him, and Justin may not even be in the sheriff's office. She hoped to hell he was, though, and had read her message. She'd know soon enough because the small sheriff's office was close.

And still the stranger stood there, staring at her. At least he hadn't moved any closer.

He closed his eyes and wiped the blood that was trickling down his face, looking down at his hand and staring at the red that streaked his skin. Megan thought she heard a sob, but couldn't be sure. Compassion welled inside her. Vagrant or not, dressed in soiled clothes and with the hood up, he didn't have to be a criminal.

"Sir? Do you need help?" She held out her hand, but he stepped closer to her and damn it, she may have had self-defense training but she wasn't stupid. If the man was hopped up on drugs, she had to stay out of reach. The door opened and Justin stepped in, all uniform and pissed-off attitude.

"Two 911s? This had better be good, Megs."

Megan inclined her head to the man Justin evidently hadn't seen in his dramatic entrance. Justin could handle himself, and he had a gun; he'd know what to do.

"What the hell?" Justin said as he assessed the situation, his hand automatically resting on his holstered weapon.

"I think it's drugs," she said loud enough for Justin to hear. The man looked at Justin and then to her, before shaking his head a little.

"No." The voice was raspy, little more than a growl. "Not those." He appeared to be struggling to talk, and he pressed his hands to each side of his head. "Just the music; Zee will know," he added, but his voice slurred, and he coughed and doubled over.

Justin pulled his weapon and held it to one side, his other hand held in front of him as he stepped closer. "Sir? Are you hurt?"

Megan saw her brother's hand on the sidearm, the other placating and suggesting and warning at the same time. She'd seen him stand like this when he broke up the fight at the drugstore. Not that he'd drawn his weapon then; he'd dealt with it by intimidation alone, because everyone involved lived in the town and no one messed with the sheriff. Megan looked at her brother, who teased her, who'd hidden her dolls and pulled her pigtails as a kid, but who was now in a situation that was serious. He was all business.

"What's your name, sir?" Justin asked.

The stranger stepped back from him, straight into a pile of notebooks this time. The shelf shuddered and some of the display tilted. The movement translated into Justin grabbing the man's hoodie to stop him falling as he flailed and attempted to stay upright.

He took a swing at Justin, who ducked and swerved. The attempted hit missed Justin by a mile, and the man followed the momentum he had begun, smacked his fist against a shelf edge, and collapsed in a heap on the floor. Then he didn't move, was absolutely still. Justin holstered his weapon and crouched next to the prone form of the hooded man, checking for a pulse and then talking into his radio.

"Dispatch, 390D, medical assistance required at Notes & Roses."

Megan didn't hear the response; she came out

from behind the counter, ending up next to her brother. The adrenaline that had flooded her to deal with this was beginning to ebb, and she went down in the same crouch. The hood had fallen back and exposed his hair. The stranger was young; maybe the same age as her, and a long cut on his temple oozed fresh blood. Thinking on her feet, she located a clean tea towel from the small kitchen in the back and as an afterthought grabbed the first aid box. There was nothing more than Band-Aids and small bandages in it, but there may be something in there to press against the wound, something sterile.

Justin took the box and the towel and pressed the cloth against the man's temple.

"Who is he?" Justin asked.

Megan frowned at the unconscious man. "I have no idea."

"What was he doing in the shop?"

Megan glanced at her brother and resisted the urge to give him a sarcastic sister-type comeback. She needed to be professional.

"He came in and stood in the 'notes' side, staring at the wall."

"And he didn't say anything?"

"Something about wanting music and the letter Z. And when I asked him if he needed help, he turned and stared at me like he didn't know where he was."

"What the hell, Megan? You talked to him?"

"Well, what was I supposed to do? He was a customer, and looked like he needed help."

"What did I tell you about drug addicts?" Justin snapped.

"The same as attackers, drunks, and anyone else who got anywhere near me, call you. I did that."

The man on the floor moved, his eyes flickering open and staring up at Justin and Megan. "I don't feel..." He never finished the sentence, his eyes closing again.

All Megan could think was, whoever he was, he had pretty eyes, the kind of blue that jumped out at you and screamed gorgeous. She couldn't see much of his face, covered as it was with a bushy beard and blood.

"Should we find his ID or something?"

"SOP is not to go searching in drug addicts' pockets," Justin said with exaggerated patience.

"You think he's a drug addict?"

The door chimed again, but it wasn't the paramedics yet. Instead her business partner and cousin, Rachel, stood in the door with her jaw dropping and the cold of the rain blustering in behind her.

"Shut the door," Justin and Megan said at the same time. Rachel closed the door with care, and her expression didn't change.

"Why is there a man lying on the floor of our shop?" she managed. Then she stepped closer, staring down at John Doe, and her eyebrows climbed before she paled and grabbed hold of the nearest display. "Shit, there's so much blood. Is he dead?" Like he'd heard her speak, the man coughed and curled in on himself on one side, muttering something, and she stumbled backward with a yelp.

"He's clearly not dead," Justin said. "Drugs, head wound, we don't know yet." Then he spoke into his radio. "Dispatch, do we have an ETA on the paramedics?"

"Three minutes out."

"Ten-four, dispatch."

"Is he bleeding out?" Rachel asked, her hand on her chest and her skin pale. Megan frowned; they really should get Rachel out of here. She'd never liked blood, not since the incident where she'd broken her arm in kindergarten and the bone had pierced the skin.

"Not enough blood for that," Justin said.

"Do we know who he is?" Rachel asked. "Should we check his wallet or something? He could be here with someone…" She glanced out the shop window as if expecting the man's friends or family to be searching for him.

"I can't look for his wallet yet," Justin explained. "SOP with suspected addicts."

"SOP?" Rachel half whispered as an aside.

"Standard operating procedure," Megan whispered back. "The guy could have needles on him."

"What about the recovery position?" Rachel pointed out. "Should we at least move him?"

Justin indicated the unconscious man with a wave of his hand. "Think he already did it himself."

Then, in silence, they stood and waited for the

paramedics to arrive and, all that time, Megan stared down at the stranger, memorizing every bump and scratch on his face. *What a waste. He could be so handsome, almost pretty, with those stunning sky eyes and the plump lips. He'd be a killer if he smiled,* she thought.

"He doesn't smell," Rachel commented, even though she wrinkled her nose. She gestured at him. "And those jeans? They're an expensive brand, you know. So he's probably not homeless."

Megan didn't feel much like discussing the unconscious man. She wanted the help to get here soon.

The paramedics arrived and, in a flurry of motion, they asked rapid questions of Megan, which she couldn't answer in full. "Did he have a fit? Did he choke?" She answered as best she could and hoped that was enough for them to have some idea what had happened. They checked John Doe's vitals, hefted him onto a gurney and left, all without the man regaining consciousness. Justin followed soon after, giving Megan a quick hug and extracting a promise from her to stay safe, and then it was Rachel and Megan alone in the shop.

Rachel looked anywhere except at the blood and Megan knew she had to get her out of the shop. "You go up to Carter's and get some fresh coffee."

"You need help," Rachel began. She looked torn as she gestured at the floor.

"I'll clear this up. Go."

"What if someone else comes in?"

"Another vagrant covered in blood?" Megan smiled as she said it. She hoped she'd had her full quota of vagrants for this year.

"You never know," Rachel said, frowning.

"Go."

Rachel looked at the door and back at Megan, as if she were expecting another strange man to come in while she was out and was worried about leaving her. Megan went back to the small storage room at the back of the store. She pulled out the mop and bucket and the cleaning supplies and, by the time she came back out, Rachel had gone. She wasn't surprised. Evidently, alongside her phobia about blood, Rachel had analyzed the situation with her rational, logical approach and had decided Megan could manage another strange man collapsing on their floor if she had to. Megan cleaned up the smears of scarlet and the tracked-in mud, and realigned all the notebooks and stationery on the knocked shelf. While she worked, all she could think was, despite the shock and drama of what had happened, the man with the beautiful sapphire eyes hadn't seemed dangerous to her.

Confused, high or drunk, desperate, traumatized, wet and muddy, maybe. But certainly not dangerous.

CHAPTER TWO

As soon as Megan saw Justin was back from the hospital, parking his Suburban outside the sheriff's office, she went out to meet him. He'd been gone three hours and a phone call to the hospital, in the hope of getting information from her aunt, the senior doctor at the health center, had come to nothing. The nurse who took the call said the doctor was with him and that was all.

"Is he okay?" she asked immediately.

"Forget him, are you okay?" Justin countered.

Megan brushed off the concern. "Tell me," she said.

"There isn't a lot to say, the docs haven't finished with him yet." Justin pulled out a pile of folders and shuffled them as he hip-checked the car door closed. "Aunt Lindsay is in today, so she's the lead."

"And they don't know what's wrong with him?"

"All they know for sure is he's got some kind of head wound and that the tox screen came back negative for drugs."

"Did you get an ID?" She shivered and wrapped her arms around herself; she'd stepped outside with only a sweatshirt to protect her from the cold. Rookie move, because Justin instantly went into pained big brother mode.

"Jesus, sis, you need a coat."

"Did you get an ID?" she persisted. "Do we know who he is?"

"Cody Brennan, California. That's all I know until I run his driver's license for a deeper check."

"Is he a tourist? What was he doing in my shop?"

Justin answered with exaggerated patience, "Again, I don't know a thing about him, or why he collapsed in your shop. The only thing I do know for sure is that he moved to town a week back."

Clarity hit her. "He bought the Evans place. That guy?"

"Yep, or so Myrtle said when she called me thirty minutes ago."

The grapevine in this town moved like wildfire and the fact their only real estate agent, in Carter Creek two miles down the river, had felt she needed to call the sheriff with information meant it had already reached the next town over. By now everyone and their families would know that the new guy in town, the one no one had actually met to talk to, the mysterious one with the beard, had collapsed in Megan and Rachel's premises. Megan could just imagine the phone calls she'd be getting from everyone who knew her, demanding the juicy details. Which, given this was a town of only three thousand souls, was a lot of people. Only in the summer, when the tourists descended, was there any semblance of privacy as locals mixed in with the visitors.

Justin must have taken her silence as something to worry about. He stepped closer and shuffled her back under the awning in front of the shop, crowding her and rubbing his hands on her arms. "You sure you're okay, sis?" He tilted her chin and checked her face to the point where it was getting a little creepy and she batted his hand away.

"He didn't get anywhere near me," she said. She was rapidly running out of patience at her big brother's interference.

"Maybe you should take the rest of the day off."

"Why?"

"Because you're likely shaken up," he said, frowning.

"God's sake, Justin, I'm okay. I can handle one semi-coherent man on my own."

"I'll come check on you later," Justin continued, like he hadn't heard a single word Megan had said.

"Justin—"

"I can't help it, okay, I saw *Dr.* Collins today and he asked me about you." The emphasis Justin put on the word doctor made Megan wince. "He was all up in my face like I owed him a conversation after what he did to you. Add in the vagrant in your shop thing and I worry, okay?"

Megan ignored the rest of the worry and focused instead on the fact that Justin had seen David Collins. *Great. Cue lots of big brother overprotective angst about Megan being taken in by the married man.*

David was the one with the wedding ring hidden in his pocket and a smooth line of seduction. He was also the reason Justin was protective of her at the moment, and she couldn't entirely blame him; but it rubbed her the wrong way that she'd been so wrong about David and that she'd had to involve Justin in getting him to leave her alone.

She'd fallen for David's innocent charm on date one, when he told her about the breakup of his marriage, fallen a little bit for him when he told her how hard he'd tried. They hadn't kissed after date one and she'd thought he was the perfect gentleman. She'd decided she was too picky, that romance wasn't all about not being able to think or breathe around the man you lusted after. They'd even managed a date two, but it was that date where he'd come across as way too perfect. What she said she liked, he liked, or even loved to the extreme. Every opinion she voiced, he agreed with. And then the morning after date two, a certain Mrs. Collins appeared on the scene, and the hidden wedding ring had slid right back on David Collins's finger.

She sighed. "Did you hurt him?"

Justin shook his head. "I managed to stop myself. But it was hard not to push the asshole into the dirt and stand on him."

"Justin, he's nothing to me, you have to leave it alone. I had two dates with him, that's all."

"You don't get it, Megs, the fucker apologized for being an asshole. He did that whole 'no one understands me' crap again."

"You have to ignore it."

And that was easier said than done, particularly when every time she saw David's smug face she wanted to hit him, and she wasn't the kind of person given to physical anger. He'd played on her ready admission that she was looking for romance and happiness and, what was worse, she had fallen for his attempt to give that to her. A strong woman with her own business, her own place, and she'd been taken in by the first guy who said things she needed to hear. She still hadn't forgiven herself for being such an idiot. Not to mention when she decided to back away, he'd continued pursuing her, even having the audacity to suggest she was overreacting. She was over it now; hell, it had been six months and counting since she'd wasted time on the flirting, the first date and all the shit that went with it.

I'm too young to be so cynical.

"Are you okay?" Justin asked.

"Stop asking me that," Megan snapped. "Sorry," she apologized with less irritation and, in its place, acceptance that Justin would never stop asking her that. Nothing was going to stop Justin, or indeed Garrett, from worrying about her. Being the baby of the family with two older brothers was always going to make her life interesting. Megan bit back the words she wanted to say, to explain to her brother how she'd felt, how she'd thought maybe this man was perfect for her, and how vulnerable that made her. She wasn't about to admit to him that she'd succumbed to the whole stereotype of nearly being twenty-five and looking for a Mr. Right. Or that, at the moment, she'd settle for a Mr. Right Now if he were available.

"You're cold, go in," he said. "We can talk later and if I hear anything about the patient I'll let you know. I'm going back to the hospital in an hour or so."

Megan opened the door to Notes & Roses and at the last moment turned to face Justin. "Thank you," she murmured. Then she shut the door behind her and welcomed the warmth on her skin.

"What did he say?" Rachel asked from her position, cross-legged on the floor. She was sorting through boxes that had arrived this morning, a selection of wrapping paper and greeting cards, but she stopped to look up at Megan expectantly.

"The man's name is Cody Brennan and he's the one that moved into the old Evans place up the hill. Other than that Justin doesn't know anything else."

"So a name then, and the fact he owns that gorgeous place with the river views."

"Yep."

Rachel raised an eyebrow in question. "You were out there a long time just for a name."

Megan sighed. "Justin was doing that whole big brother worrying about me with a side order of sheriff thing. Added to that, David cornered Justin at the hospital, so Justin went into full-on pissed-off mode."

"Justin and David in the same place? Tell me there was blood."

When the shit had hit the fan, when Justin had found out a married man had lied to his little sister, he'd told Megan he'd have David arrested on anything he could think of. Failing that, he'd shoot him. Megan had needed that kind of big brother care then, but she didn't necessarily need it from him now, nor from Rachel.

"That was months ago now, I wish everyone would leave it where it belongs," she snapped.

Rachel winced and guilt flooded Megan. "Sorry," she apologized. "My head is screwed up today."

Rachel smiled up at her and winked. "Got it, no more David."

The phone rang and it was the excuse Megan needed to stop talking about her married ex. She took an order for a delivery of flowers and, by the time she'd finished, Rachel was busy serving a customer herself.

Working on the order, her thoughts went back to Cody Brennan. A nice strong name, a man with stunning blue eyes that held so much pain. The house he'd bought was one of the oldest in town, over two hundred years old. It was solidly built with gorgeous hardwood floors and a veranda which had wonderful views of the river. The house had been empty for a year and having someone live there was a good thing because, in Megan's head, a house needed new memories.

The phone rang and five minutes later she had a delivery that needed to be done. A new mom at the hospital, flowers and balloons. Seemed like fate was telling her to get on with things. Her aunt, Rachel's mom, was in charge over there, and she shouldn't feel uncomfortable visiting, but the thought of running into Dr. David Collins was usually enough to have her getting Rachel doing deliveries. Which wasn't entirely fair because, what if Rachel were there when a trauma came in? She'd freak out at the blood.

She needed to make grow some balls, get the delivery to Maternity, *and* check in on Cody, David or no David. She couldn't stay away from the hospital because of a couple of bad dates.

Nope, this was stupid. She was growing a backbone and doing the damn delivery today. She could check in on Cody and make the delivery. And really, what were the chances that in a place that sprawling she would see David at all?

She cursed karma when the first person she saw after going through the staff doors was the one person she wanted to avoid. She had the pink and white flowers and the huge stork and teddy-shaped balloons, wincing as they bounced and squeaked against each other. Her not-so-quiet entrance was made even worse when the balloons caught on the door. Had they not, she wouldn't have been delayed and could maybe have avoided him altogether.

"Megan," David said with a broad smile as he helped her to untangle the balloons. "Delivery for Maternity?" he said, stating the obvious.

"David," was all Megan said, and sidestepped him.

"I was leaving from my shift," he explained.

"Okay." She attempted to get past him again, but the stork balloon stopped her from having enough space.

"Megan, I was going to come to the shop, hoping we could talk..." David's voice was soft and encouraging. She recognized the tone as the first she'd fallen for. Cajoling, thoughtful, hiding a million lies, or at least one massive one.

"She doesn't want to talk to you, Collins," Justin said from behind her. Megan bit back irritation at hearing her brother's voice, and surprise, as she hadn't even seen him follow her in. This wasn't going to go well.

Megan stopped and turned to face him across the empty corridor. "What is it, David?"

"You don't have to talk to him," Justin interjected.

"Justin," Megan said softly, but with enough steel to have Justin's lips tightening and his eyes narrowing in disapproval. They stared at each other for a while until, with an audible sigh, he carried on up the corridor, leaving her and David.

"I don't think your brother likes me," David said and then waited.

"You want me to tell you he likes you a lot? I'd be lying." She couldn't help her response, nor the sarcasm that dripped from her words.

"I apologized to him but it's like he hates me." David sounded like a wounded boy, as if Justin's distrust of him wasn't wholly founded.

"You think?" Megan snapped. She wished she

hadn't when David scowled. She should have shut down the line of talking by saying absolutely nothing at all. But, yet again, her back was up whenever she saw him.

"I wanted to explain about my ex-wife, but you never let me. Babe, I didn't know she was visiting," David began. He held out his hands in plea, and his tone was wheedling. "Last I saw her, she said she was leaving me. I didn't lie to you."

"David, I'm not going through this again." In fact, why was David bringing up the shit from their damp squib of a relationship-end? It had been a long time and he hadn't made any effort to talk to her since then. But now, in the space of a day, he had tried to talk to both her and Justin.

"She left me last week," he said, quickly and to the point. "Filed divorce papers, but it's okay, because that means I can try again with you and make you see we could be good together."

"David—"

"I have an interview for a position in New York, a lot more money, prestige, she'll miss out on that, and there's a space for you, if you could get over what you think happened."

Megan couldn't believe what she was hearing, and resisted the temptation to shove him, hard. "What I *think* happened? A married man lied to me, and to his wife."

David stepped forward, evidently ignoring what she was saying, like it meant nothing. "An apartment with views of the park; we could start something, and we wouldn't have to get married quickly, but I want to give them a stable family life."

Suspicion began to edge its way into Megan's thoughts. "Give who?"

David looked away briefly and she abruptly knew what he meant. His new job called for a steady married man, with the kids and the station wagon. Was that it? David glanced up at the balloons, pink with New Baby written on them.

"We could have kids," David added.

Megan turned on her heel and walked away; she wasn't listening to all this again. The job was a new thing, but the rest of it she'd heard before.

"Jesus, Megan, some women would kill to marry a doctor." A touch of exasperation and judgment slipped into his tone, like she should know better than to be turning him down. He'd been disappointed with her since she finished with him. Shaking his head, implying it was her loss.

She turned on him when she realized he was following her, the balloons bobbing around her head. If this weren't serious she'd be laughing at the whole ridiculous situation. "Leave me alone," she snapped. She was not being led down a path where she was made to feel like she was the one who'd done wrong.

"Megan."

Megan stepped close, right up in his face, and said the three words she'd been longing to say for so long. "Fuck you, David."

"There's no need to be rude," David said with that patient smile on his face.

"I haven't even started to be rude to you, but if you don't leave me alone I'll take out a restraining order," she said. With that, she hurried to deliver the balloons to the new mom, taking a moment to coo over the new baby all wrapped in pink. Then she left to find Justin. She found him in her aunt's office, talking to their aunt, gesticulating and then putting his hands on his hips. He looked pissed.

Lindsay Mercer, on the other hand, appeared tired. Her aunt had most likely been on duty all night and had walked miles along the corridors from one place to the next. The small hospital was sprawling, a result of it getting an addition every time there was enough in the budget; and the doctor on duty picked up all the cases, from teething babies to palliative care. Megan stepped in to stand next to them and Lindsay hugged her briefly.

"Is everything okay?" Lindsay asked as she stepped back, her gaze raking Megan and searching for injury or illness.

"Everything's okay. I was delivering flowers to Maternity, and decided to follow Justin up to check on the man who collapsed in our shop."

Lindsay frowned. "Like I told Justin, he's comfortable, and we're waiting for tests." Megan knew that was the most her aunt would say, but it was enough for Megan to know the man, Cody, wasn't dying. That was good news. So why was Justin pissed?

"Dr. Mercer?" a nurse appeared at the door of the office. "I have the hospital administrator on line two for you, and your coffee."

Lindsay closed her eyes briefly, took the coffee the nurse passed to her, and sat down at her desk. "Duty calls."

Megan followed Justin out of the room and pulled the door closed behind them. "Why did you look so angry when I got here?" she asked as they walked down the main corridor.

Justin looked confused for a moment, and then the confusion cleared. "Oh, that." But he didn't go on to explain.

"What?"

He opened the next door for her, and glanced around like he was telling her the biggest secret. "Your doctor is leaving."

"I know, he told me, and he's not *my* doctor, and surely that's a good thing for your blood pressure. One less guy for you to angst over where I'm concerned." And yes, she was snippy, but hell, she was pissed at being cornered by David and chafing at Justin's sarcasm.

"They're not replacing him. The board sat and decided that they only needed the one doctor at that level, changing it to a training site."

"What? They have to, Aunt Lindsay can't do it all herself. This is the only care people have for an hour in any direction."

Justin shook his head. "That's what I said to her. David may be an asshole, but apparently he's an effective doctor. With him goes the last of anyone in a support role."

"What can we do?"

"Nothing. Aunt Lindsay is taking it all in her stride as usual. Look, I have to get back, I'll walk you out."

"Who said I was leaving?" Megan said, which she regretted immediately. What was it about Justin that made her act out like a kid? "Forget I said that, but I don't need a bodyguard."

"No, I'm the one who needs looking after. The mood I'm in, you need to stop me shooting David."

A nurse passing them gave Justin a horrified look but he nodded to her, smiled, and her expression changed. She flushed and walked into a door.

Megan groaned. God save her from her overbearing brother, who had a bone-melting effect on any woman over the age of twenty.

The walk from the hospital to the shop wasn't a long one; still, by the time Megan reached Notes & Roses she was frozen to the core. All she wanted was to sit in the warmth and mull over both David being an asshole and how the hospital administrators had decided not to replace him. Rachel met her at the door with a confused expression on her face.

"You know it isn't Valentine's for like two weeks, right?"

Megan shut the door behind her and began to remove layers, starting with her bulky parka. Her florist shop wasn't exactly the warmest place—she had flowers to protect—but it was warmer than outside. The day had turned briskly icy with snow flurries that wouldn't let up, but not enough to warrant clearing the sidewalks yet.

"Yes, why?" She hung her jacket on the small hook by the door and stuffed her gloves into her pocket.

Rachel gestured. "You have a delivery."

Megan turned to where her cousin was pointing. Familiar boxes were piled neatly to one side of her counter. Two of them. She looked inside them: red roses, twelve in each box.

"Were you expecting a delivery?" Rachel frowned and glanced at the calendar on the wall.

"This isn't a delivery. This is an arrangement." She opened the top box and tilted it so Rachel could see. "All laid out."

Rachel brightened. "Is there a note? Who do you think sent them?"

Megan looked in all the regular places where there would be a card, but apart from her name on the outside of the box there was nothing personal in there.

Rachel peered over her shoulder. "No card?"

"No."

"Can't be anyone local, no one would send you flowers."

"I like roses." She could tell which shop they'd come from, the name of the florist in Coleville familiar to her.

"You should call them, isn't that Sue's shop?"

"They can stay a mystery," Megan decided. Then she pulled them all out and arranged them in a display in a beautiful crystal vase. She didn't have anyone who was interested in her, and she'd sworn off men for at least a few months after David. As to David, he'd never sent her flowers so surely he wouldn't start now. She clung to the hope that it was someone new in her life.

Somehow the roses made her feel like her day could brighten now. She'd come face-to-face with her idiot of an ex, spent time in a hospital, dealt with her snarky brother, and had a man ramble on at her about music before collapsing on the floor.

Deep breath, Megan.

Roses made everything better.

CHAPTER THREE

Cody could hear voices, but they were far away and shrouded in a fog of confusion. Phrases like "head wound" and "damaged" filtered in and around dreams of gardens and clouds and mud.

And notes. Music, with roses. Images that made no sense. And there was a woman, tall, with hair that tumbled dark and long around a strikingly beautiful face and amber eyes that didn't look through him but right at him. She was in his dreams and she kept trying to pull him out of the fog. Only he wasn't ready to let go of the cocoon yet.

"He's waking up," a voice said right next to him.

Is she here? Is she out of prison? Did she find me?

"Can someone tell Dr. Mercer?"

"Did the drug panel come back?"

"All clear, alcohol at 0.04."

"Vodka on his cornflakes?" another voice commented.

No, I had a phone call and I needed to take the edge off... that's all...

A bright light flashed in his eyes as fingers pulled

back his lids. "Pupil's reactive." This was followed by numbers and more words, and he wished even more for the fog to stay around him. He was safe inside there, where no one could hurt him, and he couldn't disappoint a single person.

"Hello, Mr. Brennan, can you hear me?"

I don't want to wake up. Go away.

"C'mon now, sweetie, open your eyes for me."

The tone changed, fewer orders, more cajoling. He liked that tone; it reminded him of his mom when he was little and nursing a fever. She was kind to him then, and this voice was being compassionate now. He opened his eyes a crack and winced at the light that poured in. He blinked again, and each time there was less brightness, and more cohesion in what he was looking at.

Fuck off. I don't want to talk.

"Hello," the friendly voice said. Cody turned his head a little to see the owner of the soothing tones, pain knifing through his neck. That was where he'd hit himself, when he'd fallen, he was sure of it. He had shady images in his thoughts of stepping onto his porch, the melted-snow-slickened wood nothing against the smooth bottoms of his favorite boots, and he was flat on his back in a second.

"I—I—don't…" *remember. I don't remember anything after that. Only notes. And roses. And amber eyes, filled with a mix of fear and compassion. And Julia Ortiz, is she out? Has she found me?*

"It's okay, Mr. Brennan, I need to ask you a couple of questions. Do you know what the date is?"

February. It's the beginning of February. Valentine's day, nearly. I think so. I don't know. "Feb'ree," he slurred. *Is that my voice? What happened to my voice?*

"And do you know your name?"

That is a stupid question; of course I know my name. It's Cody James Taylor, CJ, no, not Taylor, Brennan. Don't tell anyone it's Taylor. Brennan, like my mom.

"Cody Brennan," he forced. His voice sounded less constricted, looser, and he coughed at the sensation of blockage in his throat.

"You took a nasty fall, we think, Mr. Brennan, and have a cut on your temple that extends into your hairline, and some bruising on your throat and neck. Do you remember anything about what happened?"

"Yes," he said. The pain knifed again as he spoke and he closed his mouth. He wasn't talking again if that was what it felt like. A headache this bad reminded him of that all-night drinking session with the rest of the band after a recording event in Tulsa. Oblivion followed by a morning of praying to the porcelain god. At least he'd walked away from that one; two of his best friends ended up having doctors prodding and poking at them. That was the first night Julia had pushed things too far, the night that everything started going wrong.

Julia is in prison, it's okay.

He didn't want those memories, he wanted to know how he ended up in a hospital, and the doctor was asking questions. Along with reminding him he was Mr. Brennan with every freaking sentence.

"We need to have a look at your throat, so I'm giving you something to relax you. Mr. Brennan, do you have any allergies?"

Allergies? Cheap vodka, is all.

"No," he said as quietly as he could so he didn't have to handle the sharpness of pain in his head.

"Okay, I'll let you sleep, Mr. Brennan."

Fuck's sake, call me Cody.

The next time he woke, the fog wasn't as thick, and the pain not quite as piercing. Instead, it was more general, like his whole body had been buffeted and thrown around. Memories came with consciousness. A uniform, and those eyes, amber and focused, but they were wrong.

"The wrong eyes," he muttered to himself. The ones he wanted to focus on came with a gorgeous face, long eyelashes, and hair that was dark with a hint of red in it. Those were the right eyes.

I'm losing it.

He blinked up at the ceiling, a smooth whiteness of nothing, and focused on the smoke detector almost directly above his bed. Any minute now they'd be prodding him again, making him answer questions.

"Hello, Mr. Brennan. My name is Dr. Mercer."

"Hmmm," Cody managed, and then coughed.

"So, there's no concussion, your head scan was clear."

That was good news, right? "Cool."

"Do you have a next of kin we should be informing?"

Cody closed his eyes. His parents would freak, Zee would milk it for publicity, and Danny wasn't part of his life anymore.

"No."

"You've done some damage to your throat, we think you may have connected with something in your fall, but it's just bad bruising, more painful to you than worrying for us. I'd like to run some more tests."

And so it started all over again.

This was day two, or at least Cody imagined it was day two. There had definitely been darkness at some point and that hush that only falls in a hospital at night. He wasn't sure if he'd slept through any other days, though.

"I'm going to help you sit up."

Cody allowed himself to be manhandled. He didn't know what meds he was on, but the pain in his head was a dull roar. His throat felt looser, but his muscles were like over-cooked spaghetti.

Propped up on white pillows, he took stock of his surroundings. The room was private, the walls white, the ceiling off-white, and he couldn't quite see the floor, although he imagined that too was clinically white. Nothing broke the brightness of the room, apart from the silver of the machines. Not that he was hooked up to any of them and, even though there was a cannula on the back of his left hand, he wasn't attached to a drip. His hair flopped over his forehead and eyes as he moved – he lifted a hand to shove it back — but what he wanted to achieve in his head wasn't happening with spaghetti hands and lifeless long hair.

The nurse saw his predicament and assisted by gathering the hair and pushing it back from his face, tucking it behind his head. She didn't comment on the length of it, or the fact it hung limply around his head. And there it was: his vanity gene. He probably looked like shit. All he needed now was the paparazzi to track him down and they'd get the fucking shot of their lives. *Boy Band Bad Boy in Rehab.* Or some shit like that. They loved to alliterate when they described him, and they'd love to get a shot of "proof" of him losing his mind. According to them he was already broke—not true—dying—also not true—and angry—mostly true.

"I'll be back in five," a nurse said, as she tucked a sheet around him.

"Thank you," he said. She gifted him with a soft smile and then, leaving his door ajar, she left, her soft-soled shoes not making a sound. He waited for the next medical person to arrive, because he certainly wouldn't have visitors. CJ the bad boy with the cut and stubble would have people trying to break into the hospital for a photo, or a selfie, or a piece of him. Hell, he still had fans, even after a year. But no one was interested in Cody Brennan with the beard and the long hair.

Which made it all the more surprising when

someone, who *wasn't* a doctor or nurse, stalked into the room with purpose.

"Sheriff Campbell," the man, tall, dark haired and in uniform, introduced himself and held out a hand when he drew closer. A hand that Cody attempted to shake as firmly as his level of energy would allow. Closer to him, the amber eyes were the ones from his dreams.

"Hello," Cody said when the sheriff, all uniformed up and looking mean, didn't say anything else.

"Thought I'd come check how you were doing," Campbell offered.

"Were you the one..." How did he phrase this? "Should I be thanking you, or apologizing?"

"I was the first responder on scene," Sheriff Campbell offered cryptically, giving nothing away with his closed expression.

Scene? That sounded dramatic and Cody winced. No one had told him what had happened in full. Snippets he'd heard when people thought he was asleep added up to a whole lot of nothing. All he knew for sure was he'd fallen over at his house, smashed his phone, had the impetus to get help, and woke up in the hospital.

"Then thank you, and probably sorry as well."

The sheriff indicated the hard plastic chair next to the bed. "Mind if I sit?" he asked, even as he took a seat. Cody assumed it had been a rhetorical question.

They stared at each other in a weird kind of face off, and then the sheriff sighed. "Myrtle tells me you bought the old Evans place up on Mill Hill Road." He put a plastic bag on the bed and Cody recognized what looked like his iPhone by the scarlet case and the fact the screen was all smashed.

"A blue house," Cody said. He didn't know if it was the Evans place, but the name of the road was right. And Myrtle was the name of the real estate agent he'd been talking to.

Sheriff Campbell nodded. "Went and checked it out, got it locked up. You may want to change the locks now I've had your keys."

A few years back, and Cody would have immediately dismissed the worry of someone having keys to his place, particularly a cop. Now the thought of any vulnerability scared the living shit out of him.

"Did someone hit you?" the sheriff asked, pulling Cody out of his fears for a while.

"No," Cody said immediately. "I fell."

"Really?" The sheriff sounded like he was implying something else.

"I think there was snow, I slipped."

Seemed like that was the answer the sheriff needed, and he nodded. "Looked that way from what I saw there. So, you fell there, because you were drunk at nine a.m. I found the blood and your phone. Then, for some fool reason, you walked into town, and collapsed in a shop."

There was accusation in the sheriff's voice and Cody bristled. "Seems like it was wise I didn't take the car," he said. "And I wasn't drunk, I'd had bad news and it was one drink, not that this is any of your concern." The extra force in his voice made his throat ache, but it was worth it when Campbell lifted a brow in surprise.

The resulting silence had Cody regretting his sarcasm and hint of defensive temper, but then Campbell sat back in his chair and chuckled. Cody frowned. What the hell was this trickery now? And was the sheriff freaking laughing at him?

"Everything in this town is my concern."

"That sounds…"

"Outdated? Weird?" Campbell sighed. "It's a small town, and it's my concern when it turns out you ended up in my sister's shop, which is right next to the drugstore, which is where I assumed you thought you were going?"

Fog clouded his memories of that day as it was, but recalling why he wouldn't go to the drugstore, where he assumed he would have thought there would be help, wasn't happening. Instead the name Notes & Roses filtered through his memories and a flash of something, a sign with the name, and the idea that there were musical notes there.

Was that why he'd gone into the shop? Music?

"I assume so," he lied. Something told him he had deliberately targeted the sister's shop rather than happening to miss the pharmacy. Probably because his irrational brain was forcing him to face up to the songs in his head. Why now, after all this time, he didn't know.

"Want to tell me what bad news had you drinking not far past dawn?"

The sheriff couldn't know how much Cody wished he could open up to someone, anyone, but he couldn't. Not yet. Not until he'd handled things himself.

"No," he said, and let the sheriff come to his own conclusions.

"Your background check showed your parents, but we didn't inform them."

"My parents don't need to know." Fuck, that is the last thing he wanted; his mom and dad would be here by the next day if they thought he needed them. He was not going to expose them to more of his stupidity. And then it hit him, what the sheriff had said. "You ran a background check on me?" Shit, what if he linked Cody to CJ?

"SOP for next of kin and insurance. Dr. Mercer told me you didn't want anyone worried, your injuries were minimal, so we left it there." Campbell stood and indicated the phone. "You'll need to get over to Coleville to get that fixed. Won't be anywhere in town."

"Thank you." Cody had a spare, two in fact, but he wasn't going to tell Sheriff Campbell that. No average person had two additional iPhones, and that was one way to make it obvious he was the odd one out in this regular, small, boring, out-of-the-way safe town.

Ex-band members with enough dark memories to fuel a dozen nightmares, and who needed a place to stop running. Someone who had chosen Stanford Creek because it was quiet and small and so far away from the LA shit that at moments it felt like he was staying in a blue house on Mars.

Someone like him. Now, *that* man had two spare phones.

His next visitor was a tall man with blond hair. All smooth lines and white-coated, he introduced himself as Dr. David Collins and checked the board at the end of Cody's bed.

"You gave us quite a scare," the doctor said with a smile.

"I think I scared myself," Cody replied. He didn't like this other doctor poking around in his notes. He'd had to deal with Dr. Mercer already, and one was enough, but he could play the game of being the perfect patient if it meant he got out of here quickly.

"Stay away from the shop," the doctor said as he replaced the notes. "Wouldn't want to scare yourself again, or the woman who is about to become my fiancée."

And he left. Just like that, he gave a cryptic warning and left. At least Cody thought it was a warning. Sure sounded like one.

He owed an apology to whoever the doctor's fiancée was, and wished he recalled any of what he'd done.

He just hoped the fiancée wasn't the woman with the eyes.

But, if he was honest, the way his life was going? It probably would be.

CHAPTER FOUR

Megan listened with half an ear to what Rachel was saying as she worked on the order to the wholesalers. Her floristry business was running a very close profit margin and getting things right at this point was vital. The Smiths would be celebrating their ruby wedding anniversary in a couple of weeks and Mr. Smith always bought the biggest, fanciest bouquet. She made a note in the margin to order in more yellow roses. Mrs. Smith's favorite, if she remembered rightly. She could match many of the people in town to the flowers they liked, and it was that personal touch that made the repeat sales.

"And then the elephants attacked," Rachel announced, with an added huff.

"Sorry?" Megan asked. She looked up from her paperwork and blinked at her friend, who was no more than three feet away, with only the counter between them, her hands on her hips. She was shaking her head and had that wry smile on her face that meant she knew Megan hadn't been listening.

"I was talking about Ed. You remember Ed, tall, blond, built, nothing between his ears but an enormous something between his legs?"

Megan pushed her paperwork to one side. She certainly did remember Ed. Rachel always seemed to be attracted to the ones that were going to cause her trouble: the biker with mom issues, the bisexual ex-rodeo star with a need to drink, the bodybuilder who was arrested after supplying steroids to kids at the local high school... When was Rachel going to see that she should be dating someone more intelligent and less concerned with how big his muscles were or how *bad* his life had been?

Of course Megan was one to talk; she'd been charmed by sober, serious David who was all surface and no depth.

"He's back in town?" Megan asked. She hoped not. After all, it had been Megan who had held her when she cried, every single time.

"No, I was saying, he was spotted in Stanford Four Corners with Emily Markham, you remember her? Tits out to here, skirts up to here? Three years behind us in school." Rachel did all the gestures that accompanied the description.

"I know her." Rachel's portrayal was spot-on. She'd been gifted with the skill of mimicry that Megan both admired and cringed at. Rachel did a very good impression of David up to and including the lascivious wink he would give whenever he used to visit the shop. Rachel had never loved the idea of Megan dating him.

"They're together, he's proposed and everything."

Megan breathed an internal sigh of relief. "And she said yes?" She was relieved Rachel had missed the Ed train, but then she wondered if maybe Rachel was upset. Whatever her private thoughts on Ed, or whatever Rachel thought of David, they were always there for each other, curled on their sofa in front of a rom-com in pajamas, drinking wine and eating chocolate. There was one benefit to sharing a place with Rachel; at least both of them had shoulders to cry on if needed, or a ready smile and welcoming hug when the day had been shitty.

"Yes, not only that but her daddy's booked the Coleville Golf Course."

"Are you okay with the fact he's getting married?" The golf course was *the* place to get married around here, well, if daddy had money. Megan's idea of the perfect wedding was a quiet ceremony in her parents' backyard with fairy lights and friends.

Rachel leaned on the counter and smacked one of her hands down on Megan's. "I wasn't telling you because it upset me! Good riddance. He may have been big, but he didn't know how to use it." She smirked. "I was saying, because they'll need flowers, right? And it could be my first customer for invitations. So I saw Emily at Carter's and Kyle was talking to her, and I congratulated her and mentioned how awesome it would be if she supported some other local businesses, being as how she is so worldly and so on." She waved a hand between them, "Flowers, invites, and she's coming in tomorrow at ten."

"That's, wow, well done," Megan managed. She pulled over her diary and scribbled in the time on tomorrow's date.

"So, my point in all this was, given I got us the lead, can you cover for me this afternoon so I can work on my portfolio of invitation designs some more?" Rachel was using the puppy-dog expression, one that typically Megan didn't fall for, but today she was feeling generous. All of Rachel's designs and papers were strewn over their breakfast table, and some of them were close to being finished.

"Go for it." Megan cast a look around their empty shop; afternoons were never that busy in sleepy Stanford Creek anyway, not at this time of the year. Spring through summer and into fall the town was busy with tourists and, although the florist part of Notes & Roses wasn't busy with walk-in trade, the Notes part, the books and stationery, postcards and pens, had a steady stream of business.

Rachel near skipped away, out the door, turning left, and she waved through the windows as she went by. Megan watched her go and then went back to her figures. Only she was out of sync with what she was doing and she knew exactly why.

The idea of Emily, three years younger than her and Rachel, finding love, even with an idiot like Ed, was like a sharp poke of a reminder in the chest. Seemed to Megan her relationships lasted as long as it took her to get bored. Which was quickly, and with alarming frequency.

Was it so difficult to find a man who liked her

independence, who saw beyond her protective brothers, and actually wanted her?

Her cell vibrated and she glanced at the screen, sighing at seeing David's name and canceling the call without answering. Evidently what she'd said at the hospital was something he wasn't happy with. The chime indicating a voice mail led her to sigh again. She'd have to listen to it now, and hearing his voice asking what he'd done wrong, again, was not on her to-do list anytime soon.

She ignored the flash of guilt at not answering the call and instead focused on adding up the totals of January's orders and costs, found a ten-dollar discrepancy, and pulled out the calculator to check her figures. When the door chime sounded, she looked up and stood straight with a ready smile on her face.

Then she saw who it was and something inside her lurched with a confusing mix of interest and fear.

The man was back, Cody, the one who had collapsed in the shop. He looked pale, dressed in dark clothes like the last time, but his hoodie was not covering his head and his long hair was tied back from his face. The left side of his forehead had butterfly bandages and he looked a little unsteady on his legs. But he was standing, albeit shakily, and that was a good sign.

Shouldn't he still be in the hospital? She'd checked in with Aunt Lindsay enough times over the past two days to know he was awake and lucid but no more than that. She'd even considered visiting tomorrow morning, with flowers or something, if only to find out more about him. She certainly hadn't been told he was being discharged when she last called, which was only an hour ago.

"Hey," Cody said, and let the door shut behind him, closing out the sleeting rain and wind. There had been another snow warning and the temperature was certainly low enough for the skies to dump another few inches on the icy town.

"Hello," Megan said. Because what else could she say? She opened her mouth to ask what he was doing out of the hospital, but closed it again. Apparently he'd been allowed out, and was at least conscious this time, and asking why he was out early implied she'd been checking on him. She curled her fingers around the cell in her pocket. Even unsteady on his feet, he had an air of danger around him, anger and tension that wrapped into his pointed stare. So, the phone was there… just in case.

"May I come in?" he asked, with uncertainty in his tone. Listening to his gruff, growly voice was a pleasure she'd not forget in a hurry. *Oh, how low I've sunk.*

"Of course you can, it's a shop." She wished she hadn't said that, because it sounded sarcastic and hell, he probably didn't need that thrown at him today. "Sorry, I meant, come in, please."

He hovered there, balancing with one hand against the wall. She couldn't take her eyes off his face. Yes, there was a beard, which was one of those bushy affairs that seemed to be the trendy thing to have, but she could see cheekbones, sharp in his face, and his eyes, so damn blue they were unsettling her. Attraction pooled inside her, and something else, a healthy dose of concern.

"I wanted to apologize," he said. He looked at her with such sincerity as he pushed his hands deep into the pockets of his hoodie. "The sheriff, your brother, right? He said I scared you, and I'm sorry for that."

Two emotions warred for first place in her head. Irritation at Justin's assessment of how she'd felt, and a sudden sympathy for the man struggling to stay upright.

"You didn't scare me," she lied, because frankly, he had concerned her more than a little and the fear was swamped by that concern. She softened the words a little with an explanation. "He's that annoying older brother who would love to think that he rode to my rescue."

"Didn't he, though?" the man asked. He smiled a little, but the smile didn't reach his eyes. Still, it was a pleasant smile and one that had her imagining him without the scruffy beard.

"Didn't he what?" she asked, aware she'd lost the plot a little while contemplating things she shouldn't. She blamed Rachel's Ed story and David calling for leaving her unsettled and open to thinking weird thoughts about the stranger in her shop.

Like, for instance, was the rest of his face as stunning as his eyes, or would there be nothing but a weak chin and bad skin under the hair? And further under, a personality that sucked and deceit that would inevitably break her heart?

Whoa, where did that thought come from?

"Didn't he ride to your rescue?"

"Oh. That." She paused and considered the question. As much as she didn't want to admit it, having this guy all bloody and out of it in her shop had made her reach for her phone. So she guessed that yes, Justin had possibly ridden to her rescue. "Don't tell him," she said instead, and added a smile.

Cody sighed. "I'm sorry that happened," he began, "and I wanted to say it in person," he shifted a little and cursed under his breath, pulling one hand out of his hoodie pocket and gripping the table inside the door. His knuckles were white on the wood.

Quickly she moved to the front of the counter and held on to his arm. "You need to sit down." They had a stool behind the counter, but it was flimsy and he'd probably end up killing himself; she didn't want that on her conscience. The next best thing was the floor, but she doubted he'd want to experience that again.

"I'm okay."

"You don't look so hot."

The stranger frowned and then shook his head. "I wanted you to know I wasn't drinking, not really. I did have a drink, but it was because—you don't need to know. Look, I fell and hit my head."

"Justin said that's what happened. You don't need to explain."

He looked suddenly earnest. "I do, your mom

said she was concerned about my drinking."

Megan frowned. What did her mom have to do with this? She and Dad weren't even in town at the moment, away on their train journey across Canada for their thirtieth wedding anniversary. Last she'd heard they were somewhere in the middle of nowhere in a cabin, all loved up and looking forward to the next stage of the journey.

"Sorry?"

"Your mom, Dr. Mercer, told me how scared her daughter had been. Although I didn't understand." He pressed fingers to his temple, massaging by the stitches. "Because the sheriff said he was your brother, and the doc said…" He stopped explaining, complete confusion on his features.

The confusion cleared. "Dr. Mercer is my aunt, the sheriff is my brother, and the other girl here, Rachel, is my cousin, and she certainly wasn't scared. Intrigued more, I think." Megan watched Cody's expression change from confused to understanding. "Our family is kind of confusing."

"And then your friend, Dr. something-or-other, warned me off. So, I'm here to apologize." He widened his eyes as he swayed a little. "Shit," he cursed under his breath.

"Please, sit down."

He shrugged off her hand and stepped away, "I have a cab waiting." He indicated outside and Megan saw Harvey's cab idling at the curb. She sketched a wave and Harvey waved back. "Thank you," Cody added as an afterthought. Then he turned on his heel and shuffled the few steps to the door, as slow as an old man. When he reached the door he turned to face her. She realized she still held out her hand like she'd have been able to catch him if he fell. She dropped it quickly.

He smiled at her, a devastatingly charming and somewhat sexy smile in among that beard, a smile which hit his eyes. "I was going to get you some flowers as a sorry," he said. Then he nodded to the counter she was in front of, with the Roses sign and the word florist. "Guess I'll have to think of something else."

He let in cold air as he walked outside; she watched him get into the cab, and waited until the fascinating man with the gorgeous eyes, plump kissable lips, and cheekbones to die for, left.

Then she called Justin, who answered on the third ring. She didn't even give him a chance to say hello.

"You told the guy from my shop I was scared, you ass. I see you, and you're dead, big brother. So dead."

When she hung up she realized Cody had mentioned a doctor talking to him and warning him off, and that could only be David.

What was it with men meddling in her life?

CHAPTER FIVE

Cody locked his front door behind him and slumped into the first chair he came to, an enormous overstuffed armchair that might well be difficult for him to get out of when he needed the bathroom. Or to eat and drink. But he'd just about reached his limit for standing. Pain banded his skull and he hoped to hell the meds he'd swallowed at the small town hospital kicked in fast because, fuck, he had one hell of a headache.

The sheriff's words about changing locks came back to him as he looked at his door. He hadn't had any letters, or deliveries, or anything that indicated anyone knew where he was, but the sheriff had made him think. He added it to his mental list of things to do. The last letter had still been addressed to his former rental, and there hadn't been anything here yet. Who was threatening him, they didn't know, but Zee had someone working on it from her end. He didn't want to have to move again; he liked the house he'd bought and it had been purchased through so many different companies it would never be traced to him.

He groaned and scrubbed his eyes with his hands. Stopping in at the flower shop and apologizing had seemed like an excellent idea at the time, but he was paying for it now.

Dr. Mercer hadn't wanted him to leave, but she'd been unable to give a proper medical reason as to why he had to stay, only citing that she wanted to keep an eye on him, and that she'd prefer if he stayed in bed for at least another twenty-four hours. He'd hit his head, but had no resulting concussion. Cody had spent way too much time around lawyers not to be savvy with the loophole there. No reason to stay meant every reason to get the fuck out of Dodge.

His luck had run out when she'd cornered him by the door, all concerned and up in his face.

"I didn't add it to your notes, but I'm worried about the drinking that early in the morning."

Cody had to stifle a laugh. He'd had nights where there had been no sleep and the drinking hadn't stopped for anything as small as a need to be in bed. Of course, they'd been a long time ago, but they were still a memory he kept close to him.

"One drink, doc," he'd said with a wry smile. The smile that sold records, the one that had a million women on their knees, or chanting his name. She didn't fall for the charm; instead she pursed her lips and stared right through him.

"One drink leads to two."

Fuck knew she was perceptive. But the comment made his smile drop.

"Believe me, I know that," he replied. And then

he sidestepped her as best he could, considering he wanted to fall over.

"We do have AA meetings in Coleville."

"Jesus," he snapped and she took a step back and away from him. He realized what he'd done; let the temper inside him sneak out into his words. "Sorry, I'm sorry."

"You scared my daughter," she added, and placed a hand on his arm as he tried to move past her. He looked into her perceptive gaze and a wave of guilt had him closing his eyes briefly.

"I didn't mean to scare anyone, Doctor."

"I know," she said. "You have the details here if you need us."

I won't, he told himself. Didn't matter what she said, as soon as he left the hospital and knew he was going to apologize, he consigned the comment about the drinking to one of those boxes in his head marked *worry later.* The doctor and the sheriff had said the same thing, implying it was a crime to wake up and want vodka. *All I need is a firefighter and I'd have a trifecta of professionals worrying about me.*

If either of them had lived the life he had over the past five years then maybe they'd be drinking to numb the crap in their heads. One stupid mistimed drink. That was all. *The story of my life.*

He was finally back at the blue house he had bought for cash. The Evans place, he now knew it was called. His head scans were clear, his blood work was flawless, he needed a time-out in his own space, and he'd rest better at home than he would in the hospital.

She'd tutted at him, but he needed out of the hospital.

But he'd had to stop at the shop, Notes & Roses, to see the woman with the amber eyes. He could see where his dreams had taken a wrong turn, she had the same colored eyes as her brother, but hers were in an altogether prettier package.

His cell rang but, although he could hear it, the screen was too far gone, and he pressed the power button until the call vanished. Soon it would be out of power and he could push it away in the back of a drawer.

Which was when his second cell rang.

He reached for it on the sofa table and looked at the screen. The battery was low—he never remembered to charge the damn thing—but it was probably enough to answer. He pressed to connect and braced himself for more bad news.

"What?" he asked. No point in niceties, his agent was one of those people who didn't put much store on the polite side of conversations. To the point, like a knife to the heart, Zee Childs was a hurricane in a tiny handset.

"Jesus, CJ, answer your fricking phone," she snapped heatedly. "I left ten messages."

"My primary cell broke," Cody explained, but didn't add where he'd been for the last two days since said break. Zee was a good agent, a friend even, for she'd stayed by his side, but if she had one tiny inkling he'd been hurt she'd be at his front door. Not to mention that she'd probably bring a news crew with her to capitalize on the drama of it all. Never let it be said that Zee Childs didn't know how to make a drama out of nothing to sell records.

"Get it fixed," she snapped, "'cause, dammit, I have news."

Cody sighed. More news. More hate mail, more threats, more lawsuits? What could top the bad news of a few days back, the news that had had him swallowing a tumbler of vodka like it would make everything better?

"What the fuck now?" he snapped.

Zee tutted loudly. "Stow the bad-boy attitude; this is good news for once. I have two stations in a bidding war to get you on their sofas and talk."

Cody could imagine Zee, wild blond hair in a frizzy mess around her head, her expression permanently enthusiastic, like a perky poodle, holding out a hand in a placating gesture. But imagining her didn't make the idea she was spouting any better.

"No."

"Hear me out, babe."

"I said, no."

"CJ—"

"Cody, my name is Cody. CJ is long gone."

"Jesus fricking... CJ, Cody, whatever the frickin' hell you're calling yourself, it's a hundred thousand just to come in and talk."

"No."

"Okay, I could get them to one twenty-five."

"What is it you don't understand about no, Zee? The show would want me to tell them everything, they'd want their money's worth, and they're not paying that much money for me to sit and look pretty. I'm sorry, but everyone's had their pound of flesh, and I'm done. I told you that."

"People want your side of the story."

My side of the story? People weren't ready for his side of the story. She was still talking and he tried to catch up with what she was saying.

"…and then it all went to hell, and the money followed. Cody, look babe, Danny wants to talk to you."

Cody highly doubted his ex-best friend wanted anything to do with him, not after Cody's breakdown and the fact he'd left the band. Last time they'd actually met, in the middle of a restaurant, it had ended up with Cody on the floor staring at the ceiling, his lip split, and Danny cursing at him before turning and leaving.

Every time they met after that was with lawyers between them, hashing out how little of the band Cody was entitled to after he decided to leave. He'd wanted nothing but Zee fought for him, told him he should get something.

And all that time his bandmates—Danny, Sam, Zach, and Tyler, they'd looked at him with emotions ranging from pity to anger.

Hell, what did they want? He'd let them use the lyrics he'd written.

The pressure of being in the band, of working twenty-hour days for something he didn't enjoy, for having to live a life in the public eye, was all too much.

But Danny, he missed Danny like a lost limb.

Now he was numb to it all. For the longest time after they'd fought, he'd turn to tell Danny something, or pick up his phone to contact him, but after one attempt at reconciliation at one of the lawyer meetings, he'd backed off. Danny's anger and dismissal was the worst one of all.

Leah had died, and then the public falling out between him and Danny had served to intensify the pressure. It had been his fault. All his fault.

Fuck. I can't do this again.

He'd gone through every single stage of grief and finally succeeded in getting his head around what had happened.

"Cody, you still there?"

"Danny doesn't want to see me," Cody said with a sigh. Danny's friendship was yet another casualty of his time in the limelight. Too much of everything thrown at kids who were too young to know better, and look how it ended up. He and Danny, and the rest of his old friends in the band, were casualties in a vast marketing machine that had chewed them up and spit them out.

"You need to get yourself squared up, CJ. Danny needs you. The station is willing to sit down with Hudson Hart, meaning you as well, and the rest of them want to take up this offer of an interview. I think the boys are considering one last concert, a reunion of sorts, if you were interested."

"Fuck, no," Cody snapped. "I'm not going back, whatever I get paid."

"CJ... listen to me, the sponsors for a reunion tour will only do it if you're there—"

"Tour? You said one concert, and the answer is still no."

"Two, maybe three dates, and look, sweetheart, Danny needs the money and your support."

Cody heard the words, but they didn't make sense. Up until last July Danny had been one of the last four members of Hudson Hart, not a huge boy band, but popular enough to sell records; the last thing any of them needed was money.

"No, Zee, he can't need money." Then, without a good-bye, he ended the call before he realized she'd never said a single thing about what she'd phoned him about a few days before. Not the hate mail, or repeating she wanted to know where he was and that she'd use his cell to track him down. Nope, this was all about stripping himself bare in front of a nation hungry for any kind of gossip on the first person to leave Hudson Hart, on the one in the car accident, on the man the fans now blamed for Hudson Hart not lasting very long.

That CJ.

Silently, he sat in the chair and stared, focusing on the way the daylight mirrored the window shapes in the blackness of the TV screen. He used every single method he could to calm the hell down, but something Zee said, about Danny and money, niggled at him and stopped him from fully relaxing.

He and Danny Hudson had been closer than brothers when they were young. When Danny's brother Samuel had formed a group with the Hart twins two blocks over in their tiny dirt-road town, it was inevitable Cody would be dragged into it. He didn't realize it would become more than five boys copying Justin Timberlake dance moves in Danny's garage and turn into something much bigger.

Something that would break CJ until all that was left was retreating into himself, learning to be Cody again, and hiding in the middle of Vermont.

Danny. Of everyone in his old life, it was Danny he missed most. Just the thought of his old friend had him picking up the second cell and scrolling to Daniel's name, his thumb hovering over the entry. Instead he pressed the *i* button and looked at the date and time of their last call. March 2, 2015, the "morning after the night before." The minute, the very second, everything went to hell.

Temper snapped and hissed in him and, for a moment, he was the angry man he was trying not to be. If Danny wanted him, then he still had this number, he could be the one to ring. The idiot knew how to get hold of Cody. Frustrated with himself for letting the past back in, he threw the phone and it landed on the rug in the center of the room. A small fuming part of him wished it were as smashed as the first one, but it looked fine. Things were not going his way.

He considered eating, could see the kitchen from this position, but the idea of moving from the chair was one he wasn't happy to entertain. His body ached, his head was fuzzy, and he needed to sleep.

And when he slept the visions were there again, amber eyes and long hair, and a smile that brightened his dreams. The woman from Notes & Roses was making him think things he'd long ago put away in a box marked *someday*. That didn't explain the fact that in his dreams he did take her flowers, only the flowers were black and dying in his hands. And then there was Danny, front and center in his nightmare, shouting at him, accusing him of being a fucked-up friend, of not having the balls to get his head straight. Then the accident, the woman shouting at him, and wide staring eyes that wouldn't close.

Cody woke, drenched in sweat, to darkness, resigned at his psyche for that nowhere-near-awesome imagery of decaying flowers with the added Danny angst and car-crash horror. The Danny part he could push to one side, the crash he'd come to terms with, with the help of a counselor, but the woman in the shop? That was different. She was the first person he'd been drawn to in months, the first one he'd wanted to make a connection to, and he never got her name. He'd passed out in her shop, bled on her floor probably, and today made a weak joke about flowers. Seemed like he'd lost every bit of his mojo.

His stomach grumbled and he attempted to stand, his arms aching and his ass numb from the awkward position he'd fallen asleep in. Food first, if he could find any, a shower, and then he'd get himself into his real bed.

Food was sparse, he needed to go grocery shopping, and he added it to his mental to-do list.

Along with visiting Notes & Roses again, this time acting like he had control over himself. Rummaging through the cupboards, he saw the remainder of the vodka. He pulled it from the cabinet along with one of the glasses he'd bought at the local gas station. Four glasses for eight dollars. The cheap glasses seemed right somehow; a connection to a much older life, and tipping the vodka down the sink was a conscious decision. Too easily he could slip back to thinking drink was the way to relax, the way to chill.

His cell chimed with a text from his mom; a message that he should call as soon as he could as she and Dad were worried because he hadn't texted them for a few days. The only stable part of his life were his parents, and what had he done to them? Bought them a house with cash, allowed his dad to retire early from his job at a local packing plant, but landed them right in the middle of the Hudson Hart shit storm. He scrolled to his mom's name and connected the call.

"Hey, Mom," he said before she could launch into her patented guilt-my-son tirade about how he hadn't called. "How are you?"

"More importantly, Cody, how are you?"

Cody smiled at the tone his mom was using, half-interested, the other half cajoling. The same tone she'd used to keep him in line all his life.

"Alive," he joked, then winced when he realized what he'd said. His mom wasn't the best person to be joking with.

"Cody, please, don't say things like that."

"Sorry, Mom. I'm doing okay, I've just been busy.

The house is gorgeous, all wood and views, and I have a huge wood burner and range." He knew how to play his mom, giving her all the details that she would love. Alice and Jacob Taylor were the only two people who knew where he was in terms of being in Stanford Creek, Vermont, and he'd sent photos, which earned him at least a hundred points in her good books.

"Are you eating?" she asked.

"All the time. I'm getting fat," he lied.

"And the writing?"

"It's going well." More lies. He was getting good at this lying thing.

"I heard from Danny's mom, she said he's been trying to contact you, did he get ahold of you?"

"Not yet," Cody said. He thought of a way of lying his way out of that one but nothing came to mind quickly. "He's on my list."

"How long will you be there? Is it somewhere you are going to stay?" Unspoken was *we miss you, and we want you to come home.*

"It's beautiful here, Mom." The truth spilled out of him. "The town is in the bend of the river, and there are shops, and a supermarket, and a health center. Even a school. I think I can write here."

"Call us when you can, Cody, promise? At least every few days."

"Of course, Mom. Give my love to Dad."

"I will. Love you, Cody."

"Love you too, Mom."

Cody felt lighter when he ended the call. He'd lied a lot, but also let the genuine part of him out as well. He'd countered her worries about him eating and writing, and now he had at least a few days' grace. He deliberately pocketed his cell; there was no way he was phoning Danny, or speaking to Zee again anytime soon. That could all wait for another day, when he felt stronger, when he didn't feel like the calls would be a battle. Instead he defrosted a portion of supermarket stew, then put it into the preheated oven and set the timer, which gave him fifteen minutes for it to heat up. Fifteen minutes to get coffee, and think. Which, inevitably, was ten minutes too long. Ten minutes in which he considered the place he was staying, how he got here, what had gone wrong in his life. Then, predictably, the anger and frustration set in. By the time he got to eat his dinner, he was on a roll of self-pity and everything tasted like shit. He'd forgotten the warmth he'd felt at his mom's voice, forgotten amber eyes and the woman in the shop, and instead he was back on his painful memory journey.

What did Danny think? That he could get Zee on his side, or Mom, and they would influence Cody to phone him? Fucking Danny and his friendship—who needed friends anyway? Certainly not Cody in his self-imposed prison of the blue house in the middle of Nowhere, Vermont. The stew sat heavy in his stomach, but at least he could tick eating off the list of healthy things that adults did. *Mom would be proud.*

The shower was hooked up over the bath, the curtain fresh and startlingly white, just like the hospital. The room needed color, anything to break up the neutral tiles and porcelain. It was probably all white because it was the cheapest option in a renovation or something, but Jesus, anything but this ice.

Fuck my life, when did I turn into this moody cynical bastard who can't get his head on straight?

He stood for a moment in front of the mirror and narrowed his eyes. He'd let his stubble grow out, until it had become this beard thing that covered his face, unruly and really nasty as beards went. No wonder he scared the girls in the shop. *Not girls, women.* No one could accuse this mess in the mirror of being cute, or good-looking, or hot, or any of the million adjectives that appeared tied to his name in teen-magazine articles.

He'd never been the front man with the band; he was the tall one with the muscles who stood at the back with Danny and did most of the harmonies. His voice was good, he knew that, but never anywhere near the soaring vocals of the Hart twins. The twins were the front guys, the ones who took the group from local garage band to bigger things. But Cody had always looked good. The best clothes, perfect stubble, and eyes so blue that even he knew they were a weapon he could use to get his own way whenever he wanted.

Right now his eyes were bloodshot and his skin looked gray. His mom would smack him upside the head and feed him chicken soup. Just before siccing a counselor on him to sort his brain out.

"Nice," he muttered to no one. He tilted his head

this way and that, pulling long hair from over his left eye and tucking it behind his ear. He should chop the whole freaking mess off and lose the beard.

But then you'd be CJ again. And everyone would know you and see you and want their part of you. Stabbing you in the back, stealing your work, threatening you and the ones you love. Breaking people's hearts.

Sudden strength coursed through him as he steadied his breathing. He didn't want that self-pitying spiral anymore, he wanted to step out from everything that had happened and become the man he should be now. Maybe it was time for Cody to take himself back for real, and not let the ghosts of CJ's life overrun Cody's.

Once CJ had been a singer in a band, but he had walked away from almost everything in that part of his life. He didn't have anyone in his life now, apart from an agent who hassled him on a regular basis, and his long-suffering family. CJ didn't have friends, not real ones, not since the accident and the end of his part in Hudson Hart. Cody had parents who loved him, and a sister with a new baby; a nephew he'd never met. That Cody needed to get his act together and reconnect with the people that mattered. And maybe part of that was talking to Danny. Maybe.

"I should write a list," he murmured to his reflection. "Things to do by CJ Taylor aka Cody Brennan." He tilted his head and closed his eyes. "First, I should stop talking to myself." With a deep full-body sigh he concentrated on breathing exercises, and when he opened his eyes again he was shocked once more by the old man who stared back at him. No wonder the woman with the amber eyes had stared at him with pity. *I look like a damn hippy, or a vagrant, or worse.*

He tidied up the beard as best he could with the nail scissors in his toiletry bag, and examined the difference. That didn't work much, even if he looked marginally less like a hobo and more like Cody, songwriter and a new man. What he needed to do was visit the barber and get his hair cut.

Forget the fact that CJ, the singer and dancer, the one with the blue eyes and the broody frown, was under this mess somewhere. Nearly a year of self-imposed silence was surely enough; no one would know him as CJ Taylor. He could do this, he could let the past stay where it should be and accept this wake-up call for what it was. A reason to live again.

There had to be a barber in town, or a freelance hairdresser or something, and if he went down the hill toward the river he could visit the shop again, maybe talk to Megan, see if she caused in him the same reactions as before. This was the first time he'd wanted to seek out company, or friendship, or whatever he labeled it, and maybe she'd be in the market for a friend at least? Could they go for coffee? Not on a date or anything, but some time for him to say sorry.

Filled with a renewed sense of enthusiasm, he decided his day was organized. He would push through feeling like shit, dress warmly, and go for a walk.

The water was hot, and he shampooed his hair three times until it squeaked, the scent of tea tree filling the room. He belatedly realized he'd forgotten the stitches, and hoped like hell he hadn't wrecked Dr. Mercer's work and would have to go back to the hospital.

But if I went there, that's another excuse I could use to go to the shop and see the florist with the amber eyes. Win/win.

Sounded like a plan.

CHAPTER SIX

Much as Megan loved her coffee, it was always worth waiting for that hour between early-morning rush and lunchtime crowd, because then she wouldn't have to stand in line and she'd have the chance to catch up with her cousin. She watched Kyle manipulate all the dials and nozzles on the space-age coffee machine. Kyle was an expert in what he did, having learned his trade whilst at college in Seattle, coming home with a degree in History and a love for coffee. He'd used inheritance money to buy into this place, and Carter's Coffee, named for the family, was his baby.

"Rachel asked me to remind you to put extra marshmallows in her hot chocolate."

Kyle turned to Megan and rolled his eyes, but carefully counted out more of the tiny pieces of confectionary and added them to Rachel's drink, tutting as it nearly spilled over the top.

"And you say the same thing every time. Tell her they'll sit on her hips," he said as he put a lid on and slid it toward Megan. "Usual?"

Megan nodded. "You can tell her that, I'm not touching her marshmallow addiction with a pole.

She's your sister; you can get away with that."

Kyle glanced over as he waited for the milk to froth, his expression horrified. "And you think I can? Last time I called her out on hogging all the sweets, it was Halloween. I was seven, she was five, and she smacked me with a baseball bat. Admittedly it was from a kid's plastic set, but it hurt."

"I remember that. You had a Winnie the Pooh Band-Aid on it."

Kyle set the coffee down on the counter. "No, it was Tigger. Oh, and, talking of men…"

Megan was thrown by the change in the conversation, but Kyle had his best interrogatory expression happening and she knew exactly what this would be about. "I don't think we *were* talking about men."

"Whatever." Kyle waved off her comment. "I have two versions. Justin got all sheriffy and heroic and told me some drunken vagrant collapsed and bled dramatically all over your floor. On the other hand, Rachel told me tall, dark, bearded, and disheveled with, and I quote, 'gorgeous blue eyes,' collapsed in a romantic heap. Which of those is true and why didn't you come and find me if you needed help?"

"Tall, dark, really blue eyes, lots of hair hiding the rest." Megan touched her face as she explained. "And he was between me and the door so I couldn't get out to anyone. I called Justin with a 911-date-from-hell text."

Kyle grinned and crossed his arms over his chest. "Bet Justin loved being the protective big brother."

Now it was Megan's turn to roll her eyes. "Believe me, he more than loved it. I'll be hearing the story in every family gathering for the next five years. And, by mistake, I did a second text to a group that was Justin *and* Garrett."

Kyle brightened at Megan's mention of her middle brother. "I miss that idiot. Did you hear back from him?"

"I sent him a *no need to worry* text after the dramatic 911 thing. I haven't heard anything back, but he's probably overseas and out of contact."

"He owes me a beer," Kyle groused. "Asshole needs to come home."

"Talking of family, have you finished the catering lists we need for Mom and Dad's anniversary planning meeting?"

If Kyle cared about her change of subject he didn't comment; instead he took it in stride. Megan wasn't sure why she didn't want to talk too much about the man in the shop, but some small part of the whole situation had left her confused and weirded out a little. She clearly needed some more processing time. And as for Garrett, she hadn't seen her other brother in two months now and kind of missed the big idiot.

Kyle looked behind her briefly, then took a cloth and wiped down the surface. "Yes I have, and I'm in charge of coffees and cake for the meeting, or so Rachel tells me."

"We need to add a group gift idea to the agenda."

Kyle shook his head. "Shit, we have an actual

agenda? I thought the hotel was taking care of most of it."

"Garrett says he'll definitely be home for it and he's in charge, which means of course there's an agenda."

"Your brother needs to find a boyfriend, and then he'd quit trying to organize the rest of us," Kyle grumped. "What with his disappearing acts and organizing, and Justin's heroic dramatics, it's a wonder you're normal."

She removed the carry lid from the coffee and sipped it to reduce the level, inhaling the fresh coffee scent. She turned to leave, and walked slap bang into a wall. A wall that gave a distinctly loud curse as hot coffee splashed over the edge of her cup and onto a red shirt.

"Shit, sorry," Megan said immediately, and hoped to hell she hadn't hurt someone. She placed the drinks back on the counter and looked up at the person she'd near maimed. Words failed her as she met blue eyes and saw the owner of both the eyes and the accompanying curse was her stranger from the shop.

"It's okay," he was saying. He lifted wet material away from his body and shook it, like that was going to make any difference.

"I didn't realize anyone was behind me," she explained and grabbed a handful of napkins, helplessly patting at his hands.

"I should have coughed or something," he murmured. His voice sounded less growly today, but the butterfly bandages were a testament to what he'd been through. What if he'd heard Megan and Kyle talking about him? She could feel her face heating up.

"I realized I never introduced myself properly. I'm Cody Brennan," the man said, and held out a hand.

She took the hand and loved the tight grip, the hold, the touch of the man. In fact, she was so caught up she was slow to give him her name, and she saw the faint smile on his lips fall.

"Sorry, I'm Megan, Megan Campbell."

"I wondered," he said. "If you had the same last name as your brother, or... something." He stared right at her, the focus in his eyes unnerving.

"Campbell. Is my name. Not changing it anytime soon."

Hell, shoot me now, she thought pitifully.

"Well then, Megan, nice to meet you," Cody said.

"Hi," she responded with enough enthusiasm to get that smile back on his face.

"Your boyfriend will probably have something to say about changing names. Although I don't get that whole losing your name when you're married thing. My mom and dad did that, but in this day and age it's probably not what people do. I guess." He clamped his mouth shut like he realized he was rambling a little.

Megan attempted to follow the thread, focusing in on one thing. "Why? What?" Then the realization hit her. What exactly had David said to Cody? "You mean David?"

"Doctor, yep, he seemed very happy and

concerned, all at the same time, and implied you were his partner?"

"God no."

Cody tilted his head a little. "I shouldn't have presumed."

Megan shook her head. Then she realized they were still holding hands and released her grip, waiting for him to let go as well. He held her hand that little bit longer and when he let it go the smile was out in full force. The shape of his mouth, and the way lines crinkled at the corner of his eyes, sent liquid fire through her body and made her even more embarrassed—and hot. Up this close he was a good-looking guy, even if the beard was hiding way too much.

"Nice to meet you, Megan."

"And you," she answered. "I have… coffee," she added. *Pull yourself together, Megan Campbell.* "So I haven't seen you around town," she said. *And now I seem to be running into you all over the freaking place.*

"I bought the blue house up the hill; your brother told me it was the Evans place, if that helps."

"I know you bought it."

"You do?"

"Small town, news travels fast."

"I remember, I lived in one until I was eighteen." He smiled then, and there was a fondness at the recollection he had. For a second Megan stared at him, into his eyes, seeing the sooty lashes, so thick she was jealous, and the way the edges of his eyes crinkled with the smile. She only realized she was staring when his smile turned to a faint frown.

"Nice views," she began. "I mean, from your house; I was at school with Matt and Jamie, the Evanses' sons." She realized she was rambling and took a conscious breath to slow herself down. Of course that led to an awkward lack of words and Cody seemed happy to stand there and wait. Finally she fell back on the tried and trusted, "It's cold today and we're expecting way more snow."

"Two jackets," Cody answered, indicating the thick coat over his arm and the open sleeveless jacket he tugged over to cover the coffee stain. Guilt made Megan dip her head and she could feel her face heating.

Silence again. Megan swallowed her embarrassment. If Cody wasn't making conversation then it would need to be up to her.

"So have you moved here for work?" She asked her safest question.

"Something like that," Cody replied, enigmatic, his frown shifting again, the faint smile that replaced it faltering. Megan liked that smile; it was the only proof she had that someone real existed under the beard, under the mask of uncertainty, and she wanted it back.

"Good. Anyway, I have to go. Rachel's waiting for her marshmallows." She picked up the drinks and sidestepped Cody. "Uhm, sorry about the shirt."

Cody shrugged. "These things happen."

"Let me know if its ruined and I'll replace it or,

if... Okay, then, bye." She thought she heard Kyle chuckle behind her and her embarrassment was complete. She began to leave.

"Wait, Megan? Is there a barber in town? I haven't seen one."

She faced him again. "If you follow Chapel Road around by the school, it's there. You would have walked past it to get here from your house." Suddenly she was uncertain. How could he have missed it? Was he really alright? He still looked a little pale. "Are you okay?"

"Yeah?"

She lifted one of the carry cups to indicate her head, but it came off looking like a weird motion that implied nothing and instead probably made her look like a flailing idiot. "You should have seen it, and I'm thinking your head..."

"My head?" He looked confused, then his expression cleared. "Oh, no, I'm okay, promise. I went the long way past the school and across the park," he said with a shrug. When he shrugged like that his thinner jacket separated and the material of his wet shirt pulled tight across his chest, which served to draw attention to the muscles and all the bits of him that he hid away.

"Oh, okay, good."

"You like coffee?" he asked.

She glanced down at her cup, and then at his shirt. "Yeah, wakes me up in the morning." *Stop talking, you idiot.*

"Maybe you'd like to get a coffee another time?

With me, instead of on me," Cody said, and damn if that smile didn't reach his eyes then.

And that was her, done. She'd tripped and stumbled over the niceties like a kid, and all in front of Kyle. She would *never* live it down.

"Maybe," she murmured, and then with a quick smile she left.

She made it all the way back to Notes & Roses with the remainder of her coffee, and the chocolate, intact. Rachel took hers and lifted the lid, picking out one of the marshmallows and chewing it, a look of sheer happiness on her face. The whole time, Megan didn't move, because she couldn't, because she was mortified, and strangely turned on. She'd shut him down with the *maybe* she'd given him, and she knew it. Who did that?

"What?" Rachel asked. "Why are you bright red? What did you do?"

"I spilled coffee all over someone in Carter's, the man who collapsed in our shop. His name's Cody, and I walked into him, and he was like this immovable object, muscles and hard, and there, coffee…" Megan waved her hands. "All over his red shirt, and then he said we should have coffee and I said maybe."

Rachel narrowed her eyes at Megan. "Wait, go back a step, how *much* of an immovable object?"

Megan placed her cup on the counter and held her hands in front of her. "I swear muscles, a hard and broad chest, tall, way impressive." Even to her own ears she sounded like a teenager with the descriptions.

Eyebrow raised in disbelief, Rachel commented, "Really? Harder than Mitchell Saunders, star quarterback when you were fifteen?"

"Way harder. And he smelled so nice, like tea tree or something. And I said maybe to coffee. I mean, who the fuck says maybe, doesn't agree on a particular date for that coffee, and then runs?"

"Hmmm, you like him then?"

"There's something about him." Something intriguing, something that called to her, a protectiveness maybe? Or possibly good old-fashioned lust. And who knew she had a thing for wild bearded men?

Rachel didn't look convinced. "Even with the beard and all that hair?"

Megan was defensive; she wanted to explain what was going on in her head and why she felt so confused, but she literally came up empty-handed. Why would she feel defensive? She didn't know him other than the fact his name was Cody Brennan, and there she was, getting all flustered and stupid like a schoolkid, like she hadn't met a guy for coffee before.

He only wanted to share a drink. She could tell him all about Notes & Roses, and in turn he could tell her why he'd smelled of vodka when he'd collapsed in her shop, why he was in Stanford Creek, and why sometimes he had the look of a hunted man in his eyes.

She'd seen something in his expression, a guarded sorrow, something indefinable that bordered on confusion. And those eyes; she couldn't stop thinking about his eyes. She didn't say anything like that to Rachel though; her cousin had evidently made her mind up about Cody. How could Megan explain that she seemed to have a bizarre connection to the man that she wasn't sure *she* even understood, let alone expect Rachel to understand

The door opened and without turning Megan assumed Kyle would be coming in for her to dish the dirt. But she was wrong. It wasn't Kyle coming to tease her, or tell her that Cody had been standing behind her all the time she was chatting on about what had happened.

Nope, it was Cody himself, with a box of chocolates that he thrust out toward her. A flash of recognition hit her, but she couldn't place it, and dismissed the thought as she focused in on those piercing blue eyes.

"Figured you have flowers for every occasion at your fingertips, but failing that, chocolates are always good for an apology, right?"

She took the box and clutched it to her chest. "Thank you." Words to adequately react to the situation failed her. He was stunning, all hard angles and cheekbones to die for; add in the sapphire eyes and the soft pink lips and he could be a model. She blinked back to the here and now as Rachel stepped into their space.

"Hi, I'm Rachel." Rachel extended her hand, which Cody shook.

"Cody Brennan," he said.

"Hi, Cody, nice to see you up and standing. How are you feeling now?"

Damn Rachel with her complete control over her speech. She was asking a question that made sense and was coherent in its delivery, which was way better than Megan had managed so far.

"I'm better, thank you. Took a fall on the snow and a hit to the head is all." He let go of Rachel's hand. "I wanted to drop those in. For you both, of course. I mean, I don't know if you were here, or maybe I do, I don't remember much, but I wanted to apologize for what happened." He sounded rattled, his words a little jumbled.

Rachel smiled at him. "No worries. Your accent, West Coast right?" Rachel commented. Then she gestured. "California?"

Cody blinked like a rabbit caught in headlights.

"San Diego," he said. "I have to go."

Now he was talking to Megan, and she nodded her thanks.

"Thank you," she said.

Cody shrugged. "No biggie." Then, with nothing else, he left the shop, turning in the direction of the barber and walking away. For a second Rachel was quiet and then she put her hands on her hips.

"Damn, girl, I hope he cleans up well, because I see what you mean. That growly voice…"

"And those eyes…"

"And the muscles…"

"Uh-huh."

They watched him stop dead for a second and

part of Megan hoped he was coming back. She waited and then with mild disappointment, watched him begin to walk again and disappear up the road.

Rachel had the last word. "And did you see that ass?"

CHAPTER SEVEN

Rachel calling him as being from the West Coast was way too close for comfort, and what the hell had made him mention San Diego? What if someone put West Coast, San Diego, and Cody together, and came up with CJ Taylor? And hadn't he mentioned the fact he was from a small town to Megan? God, anyone with access to Google and half a brain could probably put two and two together.

"Small town boys hit the big time." That was only one of the headlines. Add in blue eyes and you'd be a step closer to knowing who he was.

He only understood how much he had shut down with mild panic when he realized he had stopped dead outside the pharmacy and likely looked like a complete idiot. He had to pull himself together; a few facts do not an ex-boy band member make.

Stop it. No one knows you are CJ Taylor. No one cares who you are. No one in this town wants to hurt you or your family.

Struggling to compose himself, Cody walked away from Notes & Roses as purposefully as he could. He wanted to look like he knew where he was going and had a reason to be going there. Which he did, really. He knew where the barber was now, and it was probably past time for him to do *something* with himself. And if he walked with enough purpose no one would stop and talk to him.

Well, apart from the man he'd seen in the coffee shop who was now blocking his path.

Cody came to a quick stop and for a second they danced to get past each other, or rather Cody did. On the other hand, Kyle, according to the cutesy badge on his chest, appeared to be herding Cody to the wall. Cody had no choice but to stop; after all, he was trying to fit in without too much angst, so he had to play the part, right? That didn't stop him relaxing his stance and bending a little at the knees, ready to run, ready to fight, just like he'd been shown.

Shorter than Cody, Kyle was an easy target to take out with one of Cody's self-defense moves. Fisting his hands, Cody waited for something to happen. Some accusation, or violence, or anything that was a threat. Or at worst some kind of recognition.

"Hey," Kyle said, patiently, with a smile and absolutely zero threat in his tone.

"Hey." Cody tried not to sound like he was questioning Kyle's objective in moving him to one side of the path.

"Is your shirt okay?" Kyle asked.

"It'll dry out."

"Sheriff said you live here now?" Kyle asked. Cody wasn't sure if that was an appropriate question to be asking a stranger who was a customer in your shop. But like Poplar Grove, a suburb of San Diego, this was a small town, and people knew everyone else's business.

"The blue house, the Evans place."

"Nice place. One of my closest friends is the eldest son of the Evanses."

What was it with people telling him how they knew everyone else? And why was it so much the same as the town he'd been brought up in?

"Good to know," he finally offered when Kyle didn't immediately carry on.

"So I have a few questions."

"And you couldn't have asked me them when you served me coffee?"

Kyle ignored the question. "Saw you talking to my cousin. Megan. Thought I'd have a quiet chat."

More like an interrogation, Cody thought. He thrust out his hand. "Cody Brennan."

Kyle shook his hand. "Kyle Mercer."

"Dr. Mercer's son?"

"Yep."

"Rachel's brother."

Kyle inclined his head and Cody waited to be told he'd scared Rachel and that Kyle wasn't happy about it. Instead Kyle appeared to have a very different objective.

"So, you moved in up the hill, you planning on staying long?"

"I bought the house."

"Means nothing," Kyle said with a shrug to underline the dismissal. "So how long?"

"Long enough," Cody finished cryptically. He had no idea how much time he'd be spending in Stanford Creek; maybe only as long as he was hidden, until that moment someone tracked him down. That was probably the only other answer he could think of. He'd only bought the house because he could get it through a shell company and his investment manager said it was a sound investment. Something about it being empty the last year and the owners near giving it away.

"So my sister, Rachel, works in Notes & Roses," Kyle explained. "And my mom was your doctor."

"Yes, we established that. Your mom is a good physician," he said lamely.

"I know."

"I went into the shop."

"I saw."

Jeez, Kyle was a man of few words. "To say sorry," Cody expanded. "Again."

Kyle nodded. "Okay."

Abruptly Cody was angry, not at Kyle, who was apparently a man of few words, but at himself. His first thought when Kyle had stopped him was of guilt, and he didn't deserve that. He wasn't a bad guy, just a hunted one.

"Gotta go," he said, and with a smooth move he sidestepped Kyle and carried on down the path. That wasn't his most polite interaction, but he wasn't used to sharing too many details of his life. Last time he did that he'd nearly died, so never again.

The positivity he'd felt leaving the shop had

vanished as well, and in its place was the anxiety that gripped him whenever he contemplated what to do next in this weird journey of his life. He'd decided to get himself squared out, but was that the right thing to do? If he took off the beard, and cut his hair, his CJ persona would be staring back at him, and people could recognize him. Even after two years he was still a bankable commodity, someone who could garner attention, good and bad.

He made it to the barber and walked straight in before he could second-guess himself. He was seated with a coffee before he could even offer a hello.

"What can I help you with?" the short, stocky barber asked. Cody looked at his reflection, seeing the awful mess that was him. Gone was the short hair, gone was the designer stubble and the diamond earring in his earlobe. The only thing he had left of CJ Taylor were the tattoos, and he couldn't hide them. They were all CJ. The best he could do there was to find a tattoo place and get some of them changed, or fixed or something. Not that he expected sleepy Stanford Creek to have a tattoo parlor.

"Can you…" He stopped and closed his eyes. "All of it off, grade three on the hair. All of it except maybe a longer bit at the front?"

"And the beard, sir?"

He had to battle the CJ demon at some point, may as well be now. Should he be removing it all? Maybe just trimming it?

"I don't know."

"How about we tidy it up and cut it close?"

"Okay, sounds good." He guessed he could always take more off at home if he needed to.

"Of course, sir." The barber began cutting. He introduced himself as Eddie and proceeded to tell Cody about his entire life. He even asked Cody questions, which he managed to answer, albeit vaguely with some of them. Seemed like the self-imposed isolation of the last two years hadn't stolen all of his social skills, and he managed to keep up his end of the conversation.

"You like the house?"

"It's impressive, solid, lovely views." Cody recalled all that from the virtual viewing. He'd bought the place on the strength of that alone. In fact, he'd been so determined to leave his last place that he would have bought a shack. Or stayed in a tent in the yard of a shack.

"The Evanses, that was sad. Their youngest son, Matt, he lost his life overseas in the army nearly three years back. Not sure the Evanses ever got over it. Terrible thing, to bury a child."

Oh, that was a story Cody didn't want to know. He didn't want to put names to the initials marked in the wood of the kitchen that measured heights. ME was Matt, and there was a JE as well. JE was the tallest, the last mark dated 2012, with both of them six foot at least.

"They moved to live near Jamie in Chicago a year or so ago; the house has been standing empty since."

"That's so sad," Cody sympathized.

"The good die young," Eddie offered gently.

"And he was a hero, saved lives, did the right thing."

"Still very sad."

"What is it you do?" Eddie asked as he drew the buzzing razor over Cody's head.

Do? That was a leading question, wasn't it? All Cody had done from the day he was old enough to talk had been to sing, and to dance, and to feel music. He'd learned piano, could play the guitar passably enough, but what he did best was write. Music, lyrics, words that had sold records. All of which sounded lame next to the guy who had fought for his country. Seemed like perspective had reached out and slapped him across the face.

"I'm a writer," he finally admitted.

"Oh, we had one of those up the hill some time back, wrote horror, and I don't hold much with horror, although the wife loves Stephen King. Do you know Stephen King?"

Cody stared at his reflection as the long hair fell away, and with it each moment of the hiding and the fear and the self-pity. What people saw, what the hospital had seen, was a man drunk in the morning who looked like a vagrant. CJ Taylor with all his pop star neuroses and scars. It was time to let Cody back out.

"No," he replied. "I don't know him."

"You'll get your break," Eddie said. He'd heard what Cody said and the fact he hadn't met Stephen King, and decided Cody was an aspiring *something*. And Cody was fine with that.

Lying back in the chair for the tidy-up trim of his

beard, he stared up at the ceiling before closing his eyes. His mind went straight to Megan. She'd been flustered in the coffee shop, but he put that down to her spilling coffee all over him. For the absolute first time since he'd left Hudson Hart he'd been interested in a woman and part of him, the part he'd left behind, wished her being rattled had been because of him as a man. Not only due to her embarrassment. Memories of making a girl nervous as normal-Cody had long since dimmed.

Of course, CJ had girls falling all over him, teenagers wanting to be near him, women on tap whenever he wanted them. He wasn't as popular as the twins or Sam, but he and Danny had their fair share of companionship. He hadn't hated it at all; he'd wallowed in the affection and not for one minute thought he'd ever want the ride to stop. Until the moment he did.

No one understood why he'd decided to leave an up-and-coming boy band. Who would do that? Not a single person thought he'd make anything of himself after he'd gone. And he hadn't really. He'd hidden away and tried to write music, attempted to find what was inside himself so that he could make the music he wanted. None of it worked. He'd proved everyone right. He had no talent to speak of.

Two women pulled paternity suits on him, a stalker wanted to hurt him and ended up killing someone in his care, and he had so much hate mail he moved. Then he moved again. And again.

Of course, it didn't help that Hudson Hart had

disbanded altogether and the blame for that had been put squarely at his feet. Some of the more rabid fans hated him, executives sued him.

And now he was here, in a quiet town in Vermont, where it snowed, and where people got up in his face about his business. And where no one knew Cody Brennan was actually CJ Taylor.

But, and he couldn't understand it, something about Megan made him want to tell her everything. Just to have her looking at him like maybe he had once been successful, someone people looked up to. He wanted to explain about Cody, and about how he'd pretended to be CJ for a long time, and how now he was ready to try and be himself. Maybe it was the way she didn't shy away from him even though he was a weirdo who had collapsed in her shop. Possibly she would understand the mess in his head and help him to unravel it.

So what was it that made him want to spill everything? Was it her eyes that spoke volumes, or her smile that punctuated every word she spoke? She was beautiful and quiet compassion shone from her like a beacon in his darkness. And she sparked with life and attitude and confidence, and she looked at him, even with his beard and his falling all over the place, and she didn't seem scared of him, or fazed by the shell he wore.

He sighed inwardly. Now he was getting poetic over a woman. Seemed like the Cody who strung words together for songs was coming back to the fore.

"There, all done," Eddie interrupted his musings.

Cody opened his eyes and blinked up at the ceiling, bracing himself as Eddie reset the chair.

What Cody saw in the mirror was CJ Taylor. The short hair with the spiky bit at the front, the tidy beard, the lips in a faint snarl. There in the mirror he could see the defensiveness that was all CJ, bad-boy diva.

Deliberately Cody relaxed a muscle at a time, centered himself, and the attitude in his face disappeared. There was no CJ now, no bravado, or swagger. Instead, the mirror showed a very young man with bright blue eyes and a seriously focused expression.

"Great," he murmured. "Thank you."

"Must be nice to get all that off you," Eddie said, and indicated the pile of hair on one side.

"You can't begin to know how much."

"Seems to me I read about an author that didn't shave until he finished his book." Eddie was fishing now.

"Something like that," he answered as vaguely as he had to Megan's question about his career.

He paid, and in return was given a leaflet about the yoga group Eddie's wife ran, "good for stress" according to Eddie, then he left the shop. A massive part of him wanted to go back to Notes & Roses, so Megan could see the real Cody under his disguise. He even began to turn that way, then caught sight of the sheriff walking into Megan's shop and decided he was not up to the whole narrowed-eye judging thing the sheriff had going on.

As an alternative, he pretended to check his phone and turned on his heel, heading for home. He had two missed calls, both from Zee. His agent was the last link to Hudson Hart, considering none of the guys were interested in keeping up with his life.

Of course, he hadn't exactly let them, had he? He decided to ignore the calls, but then the cell vibrated and rang in his hand, and muscle memory had him answering her just to shut up the noise.

"Hey you, fantastic news, the stations upped their offer to two hundred."

"That's freaking obscene," Cody snapped, "and it's still a no."

Zee sighed. "I told the rest of the band you'd say no. Spoke to Danny again, he wants you to call if you feel you'd like to."

"You already told me that."

"I told him he should call you. Would you answer him?"

"No."

"Jesus, CJ, he wants to apologize to you. Grow a pair and talk to him."

"Cody, my name is Cody, Zee."

And he cut off her reply, although he caught the start of it and Zee was her usual swearing self. Danny wanted to apologize, but surely they'd gone past all that. He'd called out Danny's then-girlfriend Katya, told Danny she'd come on to Cody, that she'd said she wanted to leave Danny, and all Cody had got for his troubles was a split lip. But it hadn't stopped there. Leaving Hudson Hart meant he was on the outside anyway, but it seemed to him everyone closed ranks and completely shut him out, Danny accusing him of all kinds of things, drunk much of the time. Last he'd heard, Danny and Katya had married, but Cody wasn't checking online for anything to do with the band. He was done with that, and if a twenty-year friendship was broken apart by one event, then it couldn't have been a strong relationship to start with.

Pocketing his cell, Cody stopped walking and huddled in his coat. His shirt had dried but he still felt cold. LA hadn't been cold; LA had been warmth and sun and all those things that made drinking during the day okay. Sunny, happy California wasn't the place for a brooding lyric writer to live. This here, in the cold, with the odd flake of snow swirling in front of his eyes, with snow built up against sidewalks, and the threat of more in the air, was where he wanted to be.

The snow touched my skin, a kiss... The words were there in his head, and he needed to connect with them. Snow and a kiss; clichéd or not, those were words that made sense to him.

And there was always Megan in this place, this snowy, remote town on the edge of the Connecticut River.

He warmed up with coffee, and soup, and stood in front of his mirror in just his jersey shorts for a long time, then pulled on his jeans. He turned this way and that, noticing where he'd lost weight, seeing where the dark denim hung on his hips. His stomach was flat and he still had definition but it was softer lines than the chiseled six-pack he'd had while in the band.

The only real definition he had now was on his chest and arms. Dancing had been what he was good at; all that high-energy moving with Danny and the others, singing at the same time. He'd had muscles on muscles. Experimentally, he took a few steps across the floor, attempting to find an inner rhythm to dance to, but there was nothing. Like answering the phone to Zee, his dancing was nothing more than muscle memory. Sighing, he considered what next. He needed to get out there and do something, like exercise, so he rummaged in the suitcase he hadn't unpacked, pulled out his running gear, and for the first time in two years he changed into the Nike orange. A run would be good. He'd probably only make it to the top of this road and back again, but he had to start somewhere.

The cell was dancing as it vibrated on the kitchen counter, but it stopped and Danny's name showed on the screen. So, Danny was deigning to phone him now? Zee must have told Danny what he'd said. He must know Cody didn't want to talk to him.

Determined not to let his positive vibe fade, Cody turned the cell over and stepped outside into the freezing air. He pulled his beanie down over his newly shorn hair, and walked to the sidewalk, stretching and warming up long-unused muscles. Used to be, he was captain of the track team; used to be able to run ten six-minute miles and not even breathe hard after.

Staring at the incline of Mill Hill Road, he psyched himself up, and made it nearly to the top where it split into an intersection before he realized his breathing was fucked-up and his muscles screamed for help. He jogged back downhill, much slower, settling his breathing, taking care not to push his body past where it needed to be. Next time would be easier; maybe next time he could run both ways.

And when he slumped onto his sofa, guitar in hand, having showered and eaten dinner, he felt that he'd taken an important step. One that meant something.

And tomorrow he would go and ask Megan out for an official coffee, or at least talk to her and let her see what he looked like for real, that he wasn't scary. Maybe she'd say yes, but if it was a no, then he'd live with it. He was taking back ownership of Cody, and things wouldn't be easy to start with. He hadn't asked anyone out since he'd joined the band and had women who wanted him whatever he looked like, Hudson Hart groupies who made his dating life easy.

But this was different. He hadn't felt the ice inside him melt quite so fast as when he looked at Megan.

He strummed a few chords on his guitar and just-out-of-reach lyrics sat in his mind. He pulled his notebook closer, but as soon as he let go of the guitar the words in his head fled. *Baby steps, Cody, baby steps.*

Tomorrow was another day and another chance to visit Megan in her shop; he just needed to find the excuse that made it seem like he hadn't planned it.

CHAPTER EIGHT

Megan had to bite her tongue. Emily Markham was a class-A bitch who reveled in the fact that Daddy was paying for a huge wedding and that money was no object. Several times during the meeting Megan wondered exactly why Emily was even having a meeting here in what she called a sleepy little town. Every other sentence was New York this and Chicago that; she was having the very best of everything, apparently, up to and including a handmade designer dress. Not to mention the huge diamond on her finger. Knowing Ed as she did, Megan wasn't convinced he'd bought it for her and wondered how much of Ed's generosity was funded by Daddy.

One thing Rachel was very good at, was knowing exactly what the client wanted to hear, and she was in full flow at her usual speed about summer weddings and bright vibrant colors against the diamonds and silks and who else knew what Emily was having. She talked about the value of local knowledge and of patronage by such a respectable family. Emily was eating it up, although her father looked uncomfortable.

The thing that Megan excelled at was her ability to run when she was passed the metaphorical baton, and when Rachel turned to her with the immortal words, *What do you think?* Megan already had a few designs she could imagine in her head.

"Nothing too ostentatious," she began, seeing Emily's dad's eyes narrow. Clearly he was thinking she was criticizing, but that was the way she did things. "With everything else you are organizing, you're aiming for class and perfection, so I am thinking a lot of pale colors for the service, satin and silk to match the dress, layered with lace, and with the more vibrant colors for the reception."

"She's right, Daddy, I want it to be classy, and I'm sure they can manage it." Emily sounded so convinced, but Daddy looked at her with amusement.

"Whatever you want, princess."

Shit, could this get any more clichéd? Rich daddy calling his daughter princess and paying for everything. What must he think of Ed, the barely-scraping-by ex-jock who had captured his little girl's heart?

When they were about to leave, Megan got an indication of exactly how he felt.

He leaned over and semi-whispered, "When is the last day for cancelation?"

Megan wasn't taken aback; in a way she'd been expecting it. "We'd like four weeks' notice, Mr. Markham."

"Are you coming, Daddy? It's cold."

Mr. Markham and Emily left, and Rachel joined

her at the window. "Can't see it happening," she said.

"The wedding?" Megan asked. That was the feeling she got. "I'm not an expert in love or marriage, so I can't call it."

"Ed's a mechanic who works with his hands, really blue-collar; she's a girl spending her days at her Daddy's company doing God knows what. And did you see the ring? You can't tell me Ed bought that. Hell, when we were going out he couldn't even buy me dinner."

As she began copying the details of the discussion neatly into the journal so she could type up a quote, the door opened again. Part of Megan expected it to be Mr. Markham telling them it wasn't likely Emily and Ed would make it down the aisle.

"I brought you something to drink," the voice announced from the doorway. She looked and blinked at the tall man with the proffered coffee. And then it hit her. Cody with no beard.

"Wow," Rachel said from her side of the shop. "Looking good," she added with a wolf whistle.

"You got rid of your beard," Megan said, surprise in her voice.

Cody placed the tray of drinks, three of them on the small table. "May I come in?" he asked. Just like he had last time. So polite, almost hesitant.

Megan opened her mouth to use the *it's a shop* line, but held it back.

"Is one of those for me?" Rachel asked and stepped forward.

"If you go for chocolate with extra marshmallows

and your brother Kyle runs Carter's Café, then it's yours."

Rachel put down the folders she'd been organizing and picked up the covered cup instead. "My brother loves me," she murmured.

"This is for you." Cody picked up one of the cups and held it out to Megan. She'd have to move out from behind the counter to get it and, despite still not having much control over her speech, she went around the counter and took the coffee. "Cream, one sugar, according to Kyle."

"You know Kyle then?" she finally asked after she'd taken her first burning sip.

"We met on the street, he got territorial, I told him nothing, sidestepped him and left him standing." He summarized all of that with a smile. "It's a man thing."

Silence. Megan wanted to be her normal witty self, her usual confident I-can-handle-anything self, but all she could accomplish was another sip of her coffee.

"We're celebrating," Rachel said, probably to fill the silence.

"Really?" Cody stepped further into the shop, bringing his drink with him. He wasn't in black today. He was in dark jeans, but his big parka was scarlet, and his beanie a luminous green. Not the best combination but somehow he pulled it off. She'd been positive that under the beard was a man who made those blue eyes work, and she'd been right. He was gorgeous, all hard angles and square chin with a neat and tidy short beard, and when he smiled at Rachel's chattering on about the wedding they'd secured, he had honest-to-God dimples on his face.

"...and then Megan said as it was a summer wedding she should choose vibrant oranges, and I had just the design to go with the theme, sunflowers, and it all clicked into place."

"You must be pleased."

"We've had the shop over a year now and we're doing okay, aren't we, Megs?"

Megan snapped back to the conversation, "Yes," she offered lamely.

"Started off as a small florist working locally, with me selling stationary and notebooks, you know, the notes part of Notes & Roses, but then it's expanded. We do weddings now, maybe even some event planning."

Megan glanced at her cousin and sent her the best "what the hell" look she could. They had briefly chatted about the idea of offering support in planning weddings, but to begin to verbalize it to someone who was a complete stranger was a whole different ball game.

Cody nodded again; he seemed interested in what they were talking about. Then he looked at Megan and the look was so damn focused it made her heat up from the inside out. What would it be like to have those eyes focused on her when they made love?

What? What the hell? Where did that come from?

"Are you okay?" he asked.

Megan realized he was talking to her. "I'm good."

He circled a finger in the air. "You looked a little, uhm…"

Oh my God, I totally showed all my thoughts plainly on my face. He'll know I think he's gorgeous. Oh, fuck, what if he realizes I thought about us in bed together?

"Tired, is all," Megan said. The standard answer to any query as to why she was spacing out.

He stepped a little closer, right up into her space, and peered at her uncertainly. "Are you sure?"

He was so close, she could smell the scent of him and see his skin that was pinker and paler where it had been under the beard. Too close. Way too close. She held her ground, though, and pushed back the instinct to talk. Talking wasn't a good thing right now.

"Jeez, look at the time, I have stuff to do, thanks for the chocolate," Rachel said, before disappearing into her side of the shop somewhere in the maze of stationery that she stocked. Which left Cody and Megan alone. Well, as alone as you can be when there was someone else within listening distance.

Cody cleared his throat. "Reason I came, apart from bringing you a bribe, was I was wondering if you'd like to organize that coffee? Or maybe dinner?" As Cody said this, he pulled off his beanie and pocketed it, running his hands over the buzz cut he'd had and stuffing his hands in his pockets. The whole picture was hot: the short hair, the faint stubble on his face, the large blue eyes, and the way he looked damn serious as he asked her.

"Coffee."

"Or dinner? Maybe? A guy can hope." He underlined the *aw shucks* part of that with a shy smile

"A thank you, or a sorry, or what?"

"No, like a first date," Cody said. He stepped even closer and she could smell that fresh tea tree scent again. He was too close for comfort and she took a careful step back without making it too obvious. She didn't really know this man, apart from him collapsing in her shop and the fact he had brought her chocolates and now coffee. He did the same thing, stepping back, probably sensing he'd moved too close.

"A date."

"The first one. Kyle was explaining that Carter's changes to serving dinner after six, if you wanted to do that. Tonight maybe? I don't know what time you close, but everyone needs to eat, right. I could come by and get you at six?"

Carter's, to eat, where her cousin would be watching them. Dangerous to have her family checking what she was doing but there was no way she would pass up time sitting opposite this man.

"I'll meet you there," Megan said, falling back on years of conditioning from having two older brothers, and still a little wowed by the assumption this was the first date and that he expected there would be more.

Cody did that whole smiling with his eyes thing and heat sparked inside Megan. "I'll see you at six." Then he left and the scent of tea tree lingered for the longest time after.

Rachel came out from hiding as soon as the door

closed behind him. "Megan has a date," she sang and pulled out her cell, typing furiously.

"No, don't go telling everyone."

But she was too late. Justin appeared at the door literally two minutes after the message was sent.

"You're going on a date with the vagrant guy?" he said as he stepped in. Clearly he was in sheriff mode and wasn't in the mood for pleasantries.

"Shouldn't you be working?"

Justin ignored her and pressed ahead. "You don't know him."

"That's kind of the point of dates," Megan said as patiently as she could. Justin always had something to say about her dates, more so than their father. But he seemed even more judgmental than normal in his assessment of Cody. Probably because he was mostly a stranger, but also because Justin was way too overprotective.

"We don't know who he is, or why he was so fucked-up, or any of it."

"But he's shaved his beard and he's so pretty," Rachel interrupted.

Justin looked at his cousin and the look could only be described as despairing.

"He was drinking at breakfast," Justin pointed out.

"We all have our bad days," Rachel countered.

Megan watched the byplay, wondering if there was going to be a point when she could jump in and say something about how it was her choice. She didn't get the chance when the door opened with yet another cold blast of snow. This time it was Kyle.

"So he asked you then," Kyle said.

Justin rounded on his cousin. "You knew about this?"

"No," Kyle said, with his hands up in defense and a smirk on his face. "I only told him how she has her coffee."

Justin shook his head. "I can't believe this, everyone is losing their grip."

When the door opened a third time, this time with Garrett, Megan hugged him hard. She'd missed him so much; he had a way of brightening her life with his smiles.

"You're home," Rachel said. Garrett waved the comment away in the hug.

Then Megan knew it was all going wrong when Garrett held her away from him and announced, "A date! Is he nice? Does he have a single brother?"

"With the vagrant," Justin interjected with that tone in his voice that spoke of his disapproval. Megan always thought he'd learned how to disapprove at a very young age, and nothing was going to change.

"Wait, he's a vagrant?" Garrett asked. He was unmistakably horrified and looked to Megan for clarification.

Megan counted down from five, a trick she'd learned very young growing up with Kyle and Garrett. "No," she said patiently.

"Seemed like a nice guy to me," Kyle said.

"I did think he was a criminal when I first saw him," Rachel confided.

"A criminal vagrant?" Garrett's horror was noticeably reaching epic levels. "Justin, tell me you checked him out."

"He was drunk, at nine. In the morning," Justin said, to reinforce his argument.

"Stop!" Megan raised her voice enough to stop everyone talking. "I'm having dinner with the man at Carter's. Justin can add in an extra patrol, Garrett can look in the window, and Rachel can go in and see under the pretense she's visiting, not to mention Kyle will be serving us. Now, can you all go away, or do you all want to help me wash the windows?"

Kyle was first to leave with a shrug and a wave and a *see you later.* Rachel disappeared behind her displays, and Justin huffed out with a black cloud over his head, muttering something about deeper background checks, drugs, and gangs. Which just left Garrett. The middle sibling in the Campbell family, he was the peacemaker between icy Justin and fiery Megan. Well, usually fiery Megan, not so much these last few days. Megan blamed Cody for her lack of witty comebacks and put-downs.

They hugged again, this time for longer, and Garrett pulled the stool around to sit on it.

"So you're home then," Megan commented. Last she'd seen her brother was before Christmas. He had a sales job that took him all over the world, something to do with pharmaceuticals and his chemistry degree.

"Good timing, I think," he said with a smile, and promptly stole her coffee, sighing in pleasure as he drank from the cup.

"For how long this time?" she asked. No doubt about it, she missed Garrett when he wasn't here.

"A week or so maybe," he said with a smile. "Enough about my plans. Tell me all about this vagrant guy you're dating," he said, and leaned against the counter to emphasize that he wasn't going anywhere until Megan spilled everything. Having a perceptive, supportive brother was a good thing; they could share talking about boys from a male perspective, but it was also a bad thing, because Garrett had a patented way of pulling out every single one of Megan's worries and insecurities. He always said she should assess a man before she jumped into bed with him, that it was his job to look out for her.

Seemed to her that between Garrett and Justin she was never going to have a long-term relationship with anyone both her brothers approved of.

Megan sighed noisily. However she explained this it was going to make her sound insane. "He's the guy who collapsed in the shop, and don't tell me you haven't heard all about that."

Garrett side-eyed her. "Justin may have texted me after I called him. You did 911 me, you know, which eventually reached me last night when I landed along with your apology text."

"Sorry to worry you."

Garrett leaned over and cupped her face, looking her straight in the eyes. "Justin said I didn't need to worry."

"You didn't text *me* back or call *me*, but you contacted Justin."

For a second Garrett looked uncomfortable, and then the familiar smirk reappeared. "Big brother business." But, one thing, never be sorry for texting me," he murmured. Then he ruined what could have been a very close moment by pressing a noisy kiss to her forehead.

"Ass," Megan snapped, and wiped her skin with the sleeve of her top.

"So, this guy, he's the one Aunt Lindsay patched up?"

"Him, yes."

"And he's nice? As alcoholic vagrants go?"

Megan sighed. "I don't know about nice; he bought chocolates and coffee and he's said sorry so many times, not to mention he's gorgeous, and has these beautiful eyes, and he's fit and tall."

Garrett laughed. "You had me at gorgeous, sis. My advice, if you want it?" He paused and she nodded. "Meet him at six, and have fun."

He pulled Megan in for a hug, and then added in a softer tone that only she could hear, "But if he's a waste of space Justin and I *will* kill him. Slowly." He backed away. "I'm staying with Kyle."

Megan couldn't understand why he was the only one of the five cousins who hadn't invested the inheritance from their grandparents into bricks and mortar the same as the rest of them had.

"You should get your own place, you know, for when you come back to town."

His smile faltered a little. "Maybe, one day. Meanwhile, Kyle is doing lasagna tonight." He rubbed his stomach as he waggled his eyebrows, then found Rachel on her side of the store, hugged her, and left. Garrett had a way of sweeping into a place, pulling everything together, and making things seem less bleak.

Smiling, Megan concentrated on the Smiths' bouquet, losing herself in roses and ribbons, planning to get upstairs by five, have a shower.

"You need to stop working by five," Rachel voiced Megan's thoughts as she appeared from the small stockroom holding all her supplies.

"I am."

"What are you wearing?"

Megan set the wire to one side of the ribbons and carefully placed the box of sunshine-yellow roses on the desktop. She could lose herself in her designs, in the flowers that spoke to her, but found she needed the interruption so she wouldn't focus on how tonight might be a bad thing.

"I'll find something," she murmured as she considered where to start.

"You're absolutely no fun," Rachel groused. Then she placed her elbows on the counter and sighed. "He was stunning, all model-like and strong-chinned with that cute beard thing."

"Strong chinned."

"It's a thing you know," Rachel said with a huff. "Add in long hair and—"

"He took his beanie off and he's cut his hair. All of it."

Rachel fake pouted. "I liked him better with long hair."

Megan looked up at Rachel. "You wouldn't say that if you saw him. He looked good, so very, very good. A bit pale still, not so gray, but he had these dimples…"

"I noticed."

They grinned at each other, but it was Rachel who had the last word. "We are so shallow."

They worked side by side, a few customers coming in for flower orders; a group of schoolchildren in looking at notebooks; other than that it was a slow afternoon.

"What is that man doing?" Rachel said, a little after the middle of the afternoon coffee run.

"What man?"

"He's taking photos of the shop."

That was nothing new, the main street of Stanford Creek was pretty with awnings and old brick, but there must have been something different about this if Rachel was commenting on it. Megan saw him on the opposite side of the street, his back to the river. He had a camera and a clipboard and was juggling both, before crossing the street and making his way directly to them. He pushed open the door and smiled.

"Afternoon ladies, mind if I take some measurements while I'm here?"

Megan looked to Rachel, who appeared as dumbfounded as she was. "Why?" Rachel finally asked.

"For the listing," he explained. Then he fished a card from his pocket. "My name is Andrew Rettin, and I'm with Coleville Commercial, here to work on listing the shop for sale."

"It's not for sale," Megan said immediately.

Andrew frowned and checked his information. "Notes & Roses; owner called for an appraisal."

"We're the owners," Megan said.

"What the hell?" Rachel added.

A sudden understanding smile cleared Andrew's frown. "Ah, it's probably the building owners who are looking to sell. They said something to our receptionist about one of the people in the shop relocating to the city?"

"No," Megan said.

His smile fell. "Sorry, if they are selling then this isn't a good way to find out."

Rachel looked pointedly at Megan.

"It's ours," Megan said. "We own the building. So I think you're mistaken."

Andrew looked down at his notes, visibly flustered. "I don't understand. I'll check with the office and our contact who booked the valuation." He traced the information with his finger, tutted and shook his head. "I really do apologize, I have no contact information on here, I think the office sent me without checking details."

"It's okay," Rachel said cheerfully as she ushered him out the door. "Weird," she added as she watched him walk down the road.

When their great-grandparents died, each of the five cousins was left a pot of money. Justin put his into a house, Kyle into the café, Garrett had his in investments—or so he said—and Rachel and Megan had decided to buy the run-down property next to the drugstore. Their money, and their hearts, were tied into this place. Still Megan had to ask.

"Do you want to sell? Did you ask an agent to assess for sale?"

Rachel looked a little hurt, then equally as inquisitive. "No. Do you want to sell? Did you ask them?"

"God, no. I love what we have here."

Rachel hugged her hard and when she pulled back she was smiling. "Then it's a stupid mistake."

Still, mistake or not, Megan was unsettled, and she didn't know who or what to blame. She put it down to thinking about the date tonight and concentrated back on work.

And through all of it she couldn't get Cody out of her head, alternating between concern and a healthy amount of interest.

This could be the worst thing she'd ever agreed to, was what her head told her. Her body, however, was all for up close and personal with the intriguing man.

By the time it was five and time to shut the shop for the night, she was a mess of nerves. She hardly knew Cody, not much past his name and where he was from, and that he'd bought a place in town.

Anticipation helped her through showering, deciding what to wear, and finishing her makeup. She lined her eyes in a subtle gray, used a pale gold to highlight the arches, and kept her lipstick neutral.

Finally happy with the way she looked, in her newest jeans and a lilac shirt, it was excitement that gripped her as she walked out to show the work to Rachel, who smiled and tried for a wolf whistle.

"Looking good, girl, looking good."

CHAPTER NINE

Cody had hours to kill and for a while he contemplated going for a run, only looking at the new snow falling, he decided it wasn't a good time. He thought about cleaning up his house, but it wasn't that untidy in reality. He even pulled out his notebook and guitar but there was no inspiration there; no love in his heart.

He had two more missed calls from Danny and the cell sat to the side in the kitchen, the big *2* next to Danny's name accusing. He picked up the cell to call at least three times, and then placed it back down each time. He'd call after the next coffee. After he'd taken out the trash. After he'd had a shower.

And then it was time to get ready for the date, and there was no time left to call Danny. This was avoidance at its best, but tonight he didn't want the past intruding. Hell, not just today; any day.

He stood in front of his meager selection of clothes and, for the first time in a long time, he thought about his closet at home, his last home, the one he'd left in a hurry six months back. He'd had so many clothes he didn't know what to do with them. Turns out you get rich and famous enough to afford the labels and they get given to you for free so you could be seen wearing the latest in designer fashion.

But in this closet? Nothing but what he'd managed to stuff in two cases. Some newish jeans, one shirt that was neat and clean.

"What a comedown," Cody muttered. Then it hit him so hard he sat on the edge of the bed. This was the first time in over a year that he'd cared what he looked like. Was it a good thing? Was he channeling CJ? "I don't want that."

Critically he eyed the rest of what he could see. Dark pants hung to the right, a blue T-shirt on the left and, somewhere in the drawers there was a dark blue sweater that had been what he was wearing when he'd left San Diego in the dead of night.

That would work.

He towel dried and caught sight of himself in the mirror. The shock of seeing his head with hardly any hair was one he wasn't getting used to. He'd poured shampoo into his hand and washed most of it off with water. Short hair was so easy to deal with.

"And now you sound old."

Finally dressed, he realized he was ready an entire hour before meeting Megan. Carter's Café was less than ten minutes' walk and he idly picked up his guitar, standing by the back window. He'd known nothing about this house when he bought it. Vermont, as far away from anyone as possible, in a decent house where they'd take cash, had meant that he was now in a place where, for the first time in a long while, he felt there could be peace.

The view from the place down to the river, with the hills beyond, was beautiful in daylight, although partially obscured by a huge growth of green that needed taming. He should add it to his list of chores. The removal of the foliage meant more view, which equated to more money when he came to sell. Because, after all, he was going to be selling. Someone would let slip where he was, that was inevitable, and not helped by the fact he'd put himself in the hospital. He settled the strap of the guitar over his shoulder and, not for the first time, wished his piano were here. He had a love-hate relationship with the guitar, particularly now when the block in his head was like a freaking brick wall. He strummed a chord, then stopped, his fingers on the strings in a G. He hummed the note and rested his forehead on the window, watching the soft snow falling, lazily drifting past the glass, creating a mesmerizing dance that helped him focus.

All the noise of the world, Danny's call, Zee's insistence that he should get back in the saddle, it all disappeared and he hummed the first few lines of one of Hudson Hart's hits; one that he'd written lyrics for before he'd left. The music was all Tyler, though. Easily the more musical of the twins, he and Cody had spent hours over this song, harmonizing voices, finding the right words and the right notes. The humming turned to singing, and he slowed the words to a melancholy refrain that matched the snow, realizing he recalled every single nuance of the music, acknowledging he would never lose it.

Sadness overwhelmed him, followed swiftly by a brief uncertainty of what he was doing here. A glance at his watch showed him he still had half an hour to go, but he needed to get out of the house. He laid his guitar carefully on the sofa and straightened, calling on every breathing technique he had to stop the feeling of being out of control. He wasn't CJ Taylor anymore, he wasn't in danger here, and no one even knew him anymore. He had to remember that.

The paths were slippery with the white stuff and that slowed down the walk, but he was at Carter's with time to spare. When he opened the door, the air was still redolent with the scents of coffee but with an added soft hint of tomatoes and garlic teasing his nostrils. The menu he'd seen on the door for after-six dining was Italian in theme, with pasta and pizzas, and the lighting was dimmer than he recalled. There were signs of the coffee shop, but whoever had worked on setting up for the evening had made the place look less shop and more restaurant.

Kyle stood just inside the door, a large box in his hands.

"I have a table booked for two," Cody said quickly, before Kyle could do another interrogation as he had on the street.

"Come with me."

Cody followed Kyle past the tables by the counter and, through an arch he hadn't spotted before, to a secluded area of the restaurant. Kyle gestured to the table right in the corner and Cody took the seat facing the arch. "I should imagine Megan is running late,"

Kyle said with a welcoming, not at all threatening, smile.

"I'm early," Cody explained.

Kyle smiled and that smile was so damn familiar. There was a definite family resemblance in the way he and Megan smiled. "She's always late."

Cody nodded. He couldn't exactly get his head around the small town thing, where everyone seemed to be invested in Megan's life. From Kyle and Rachel the cousins, to Justin the brother, it seemed as if there was an awful lot of Megan's family to worry about her.

"Would you like something to drink?" Kyle asked.

"Water for now."

Kyle nodded and there was a light of approval in his eyes. The funny thing was, Cody felt warmth at that approval, like it meant something to him. Go figure.

Kyle disappeared through the rear swing door, and was back quickly with water, placing it in front of Cody. Then he did something Cody wasn't expecting. He slid into the chair opposite. Cody wasn't sure what to do and neither did he actually know where to look.

"So you asked Megan to dinner," Kyle started. He'd steepled his hands, with his elbows firmly on the table, and there were questions in his eyes. Was this how small towns handled information gathering? Sitting and demanding answers? Cody nearly looked around for the spotlight he was sure was pointing at him.

"Yes," he answered, when what he wanted to do was inquire as to why the hell Kyle thought it was okay to sit and interrogate him. No way was he backing down, however much Kyle decided it was his place to make sure Cody fit whatever criteria Kyle had in his head for someone who wanted to date Megan.

"Justin tells me you bought the Evans place. He's the sheriff. Justin, I mean, not Jim Evans who owned the house, or Barbara, his wife."

Cody took a few seconds to work his way through the sentence. "I did."

"It was on the market for offers over four hundred; he said you bought it cash."

"I'm sorry?" Hang on now, what was the sheriff doing with knowledge like that, and how the hell did Kyle now know?

"It's okay, it's a solid house, and Myrtle, the real estate agent, is a family friend. She said she didn't know who was buying it, that she was worried whoever bought it might not be a good owner."

"She did?" A bunch of companies went through the motions to get him this property.

"She said there was too much sadness in the house for a wrong owner to handle. So karma picked you and you don't seem too bad."

He didn't have time to answer before Kyle moved rapidly on to the next subject.

"Rachel said you weren't a vagrant, although I think Justin is worried, like we all are, about the drinking."

Jesus, what the hell?

"You look really young, how old are you exactly?"

Cody didn't want to answer, but he felt like if he didn't then Justin would be arriving, and between him and Kyle, Cody would be out of luck with Megan. The feeling wasn't a good one and he was beginning to work past annoyed to severely pissed off. "Twenty-five."

"And do you have a job?"

"Kyle!" Megan snapped from behind him. "Leave him alone."

Cody snapped out of his downward spiral of asking what the fuck was happening here and his gaze locked with a newly arrived Megan, who stood at the arch with her arms crossed over her chest.

Kyle looked momentarily guilty, then stood with a grin on his face and pulled Megan, crossed arms and all, into a hug. He whispered something and Megan shook her head with a look of affectionate despair on her face.

"No, Kyle, I won't, and yes, Kyle, I will."

Cody blinked at the curious answers Megan had given her cousin. He stood to welcome Megan, and Kyle vanished with one last pointed glance at Cody. Megan approached the table, shucking off her jacket and running fingers through her long dark hair, which was damp, probably from the snow. He wondered how far she had walked to get here. Did she live close?

She slid into the vacant chair and Cody sat as well.

"Sorry about Kyle," she said with a wry smile and a shake of her head.

"Nothing I can't handle. I'm only hoping that's the last cross-examination."

"What did he ask you?"

"There was less asking, and more telling," Cody summarized. "Rachel says I'm not a vagrant, Justin, who is the sheriff, has apparently talked to someone about how I bought the house, and is also worried about my drinking. Although, it seems your entire family is troubled about that. I would point out that before that morning I hadn't drunk in months, I drink socially, and it isn't the answer to all my troubles." He stopped talking, aware that he was coming off as defensive. That wouldn't go down well, surely.

Megan winced. "Sorry. They're all kind of protective."

"I get protective older brothers."

"And cousins. The last guy I dated was a loser; you met him, at the hospital," she offered quietly, and then grimaced. "Not that I'm assuming this is an actual date, even after what you joked. I didn't mean—"

"Oh, I thought it was a date," Cody interrupted to correct her. Megan looked directly at him and smiled.

"Okay then," she said after a short pause.

"Anyway, they can ask me all the questions under the sun, but I'm not sure there's a lot left about me you won't know." He knew he was lying, but he wanted the flow of the conversation to continue.

"Well, I know you bought the Evans place for cash," she said, counting off on her fingers. "Justin came into the shop and told me that. Of course, he hinted it was because you might be a drug dealer, or something similar." She smiled as she spoke and Cody began to relax slowly.

"He doesn't have a high opinion of me, does he?"

"Well, then there's Kyle who says that, even though he's as concerned about the drinking as Justin, you don't seem to be much like a drug dealer to him."

"I'll thank him when he comes back with food."

She smiled at him, her amber eyes lighting with mischief. The expression looked good on her and all he wanted to do was haul her across the table and kiss her.

Right now. In the middle of this empty place, possibly even with Kyle watching, he wanted to kiss her, and hold her.

Desire washed over him and it confused him at first. This strength of feeling for a person he'd only recently met was overwhelming. But a kiss wasn't likely if her family had decided he was an alcoholic drug-dealing vagrant.

Didn't matter what any of them thought, he was a good man underneath everything else and he was damned if he was going to have her thinking anything else.

"Of course, Rachel is kind of stuck in the Cody-can-do-no-wrong loop, which is her normal default position. Once she's convinced of something, my cousin is way too trusting."

"So I'm batting one out of three?" Cody leaned back in his chair.

"You're lucky it's one," she said, then she smirked a little. "Actually it's one out of four."

"Who else doesn't like me?" Cody said with exaggerated horror and hand to his chest.

"It's Garrett you need to watch out for."

"Garrett?"

"My other brother. You haven't met him yet."

"I'll try to make a better impression on him than I did on Justin. Coming over like a drug dealer isn't a good start."

"You can't be as bad as my ex."

Cody didn't imagine anything could be worse than taking a dive in front of her brother, and he huffed a laugh. "The doctor? Good to know."

The doctor had said he was almost engaged to Megan. He'd lied, but that didn't mean he was a complete waste of space, he was maybe territorial? Seemed like most of the men in town were, in some way or another. He didn't want to ask, because tonight wasn't about what happened before, it was about having fun and flirting and maybe some kissing and who knew what else. He was hard just thinking about it, and he shifted a little in his seat.

"You okay?" she asked. "Kyle is talking about making the evening service a real thing but he'll have to invest in better chairs if he wants clients to sit for longer than thirty minutes."

"This isn't a permanent thing then?" Cody asked, aware he wasn't clear, and qualifying it with a wave of his hand around him.

"You mean the dinners? To locals, yes, Kyle opens up maybe three nights a week, tonight one of them. He loves cooking and he wants to offer this service as standard. I know he's looking for help to get it off the ground. It gets busy later, around eight or so."

"Are there menus?"

"No, he cooks whatever he thinks people would like. Pretty much potluck, but Garrett mentioned he was getting lasagna so I imagine that's what it will be. Garrett and Kyle are super close and Garrett is staying up in Kyle's apartment while he's in town."

"I like Stanford Creek, it has a good feel to it."

Megan smiled. "We try our best."

"Have you always wanted to be a florist?" Cody chose the best conversation starter he could. She seemed so at home in the shop, among her flowers, and the vibe he got in Notes & Roses was a good one, despite how he'd collapsed there on his first visit into town.

"I kind of fell into it. To cut a long story short, I was at college studying art history, and ended up getting a part-time job at a florists' just off campus. At first it was delivering, clearing up, but I was interested, and the woman who owned it noticed I was asking questions, so she showed me some things. I never imagined it as a career but, when the chance came to buy a shop in town with Rachel, it was the obvious choice. I love what I do, sharing all the emotions with the town; the happy times, the sad times. I feel like it's the right place for me to be."

"It suits you," he said. "You look happy." He changed the subject. "It must be nice sharing a space with your cousin. I like her."

Megan huffed a laugh, "She says it like it is, and she's good for me."

"Must be that every time you move there is a member of your family underfoot."

"Tell me about it. You've seen firsthand how close we all are geographically. Apart from Garrett, who has a job working for a pharmaceutical company and is always out of town. But when he's back, it's like being a kid again with your cousins and siblings all up in your business." She had a fond look on her face and Cody imagined it wasn't as hard as all that. To have so many people around that looked out for you.

"And you're moving into wedding planning?"

"We talked about it; Rachel is the organizer, the one with all the ideas. It's her fault I'm in the shop; well, not fault, but all five of us came into an inheritance at the same time and she suggested we buy the place outright and make something that would last."

An inheritance implied something awful had happened. Cody decided the first date wasn't the place to dig into what. He was happy to watch Megan talk, feeling equally at peace and utterly enamored all at the same time.

She looked directly at him and quirked an eyebrow, giving the impression she was reacting to the expression on his face. He wondered how focused he looked.

She indicated him with a wave of her hand, her nails painted a wild lavender color that matched her shirt. "So you know I own and run a florist and stationery shop with Rachel; what is it you do?"

"I'm a songwriter, currently mildly successful, with enough money saved to buy a house." He thought that would cover all the bases.

Megan leaned forward. "A songwriter? That's so cool. Who have you written for?"

Cody thought on his feet, recalling one of his songs that had been bought by the most obscure band ever. "You like death metal?"

Megan frowned. "No."

Cody's answer to that was to shrug. "See, mildly successful is pretty much where I fit."

"What inspires your lyrics? I guess it's like writing poetry, or at least that is how I imagine it."

"Pictures, life, music, people, nature. Anything, really."

"And you write lyrics for death metal bands? Do these bands actually sing about nature and life?"

"You'd be surprised," Cody answered. He used a smile to underline the words and she smiled back, her soft lips curving just right, and the smile reaching her beautiful eyes.

Kyle reappeared to deliver hot plates of rich-smelling lasagna, and his arrival interrupted the smooth flow of conversation. Cody didn't care what was put in front of him; he wanted to keep talking to

Megan. She made him smile, and he needed to smile. She didn't pry into who he was, but telling her who he had been for the last few years was on the tip of his tongue. What would it hurt for her to know who he was? She didn't strike him as someone who would betray him. She was open and honest and funny, and that was the furthest away from all his exes as it could get. But, for every thought he had of being honest, he had another that said he should wait and see. So he didn't a say a thing about CJ; he talked about singing, dancing, and writing, and Cody allowed himself to feel the love for what he did, and for what he could do. He couldn't stop himself smiling.

"Evening." A man's voice snapped him out of his happy place and he started. Hell, he hadn't even heard the guy approach.

"Garrett, not now," Megan said tiredly.

"I'm Garrett." The tall scary-looking guy held out a hand, and Cody dropped his knife to shake hands. He was tall and gripped harder than Justin did. He shared the same amber eyes as both Justin and Megan, and his hair was ruthlessly short. If he didn't know that Garrett had a career in sales, he would have put him as a cop like his brother.

"Cody," he said, and made to stand.

Garrett waved him to stay sitting. "Checking in on my little sister," he said, with heavy meaning.

Then with a press of a kiss to the top of Megan's head, he went through the staff doors.

"Sorry," Megan began. "He was coming to get dinner—"

"Megan, hey, did you see Garrett come in here?"

Cody looked up again. This time it was Justin, who stood with his arms folded over his chest.

"Justin, you know, for heaven's sake, that he just walked through here."

"Cody." Justin nodded to Cody.

"Sheriff."

"Call me Justin. Nice lasagna?" Justin asked. Cody got the sense he was asking something else. Something deep and meaningful that included a whole lot of warning about looking after Megan. He recalled Robert De Niro's character in *Meet the Fockers*, with his circle of trust. He wondered how long it would take to earn a place inside Justin's circle, if ever. And whether he'd make it alive.

Justin left, with the same affectionate kiss to Megan's head. All she could do was narrow her eyes at him and then shake her head.

"I swear, if Rachel comes in here I will stab her with my fork," she muttered after her retreating brother.

"Aww," Cody said with a smile. "They're looking out for you, sitting with the vagrant." He widened the smile and finally she cracked her own smile, shaking her head at the same time.

"I know. Still irritates the hell out of me. Anyway, back to you saying you could dance. For real? My brother's dancing is a sight to behold, a lot of posing and flailing and only at weddings after beer."

"I do okay." If she'd seen him when he'd tried a few moves earlier she would have laughed, but he'd get it back again. When Hudson Hart had started he'd been passable, able to swing a little from left to right and strike all the right poses in time with the music, but by the time he'd left he had dance moves that he never thought he'd manage.

"And sing." She was pressing for more.

"Passably," he said with a smile. He was no Sam or Zach, but he'd held his own on tour.

"Sing me something," she said, leaning forward to get closer to him.

He swallowed. This close he could see the striations in her amber eyes, flecks of dark brown and gold, and long lashes that swept up as she looked at him. Sing her something? Like what? His mind was a blank, and all he could think of was the same song he'd been singing earlier. But that was a Hudson Hart song and he wasn't going to do that in front of her. Instead he shook his head.

"Dancing is date six, singing I leave for date eight."

"What if we don't make it past date one?" she teased.

He leaned in as she had done and they were close enough that they could kiss if they wanted. He didn't push for a kiss, but he did smile. "I'd like to think we'll make it to two, at least," he whispered.

"You'd better pull out all your best moves then," Megan said.

They were going to kiss, he wanted to kiss her, and they were so close he could nearly taste her. What would their kisses be like? Would she be shy? Would he be able to control the need to kiss her until she knew nothing but his kisses? The tension was thick and she tilted her head a little, her pupils growing larger as he drew closer.

"Everything okay?" Kyle asked. He was smiling at them both, and picked up the plates.

"Thank you," Cody said automatically. "It was really good."

"Sorry to interrupt whatever you were doing." Kyle smirked.

"Kyle," Megan warned.

"What? You seemed like you were... talking," Kyle said, his grin replaced by an innocent expression. "Dessert?"

Cody looked to Megan, but she shook her head. All he knew was that he wanted to go somewhere to kiss Megan. Just one kiss. Just to see...

Cody would never know whether they would have kissed at that moment, at the table. He almost hoped not; he wanted the first kiss to be entirely private, and he had no doubt there would be a first kiss.

"Seriously," Megan began. "The next date has to be somewhere there is no family, at all."

The food had been lovely, the company even more so. And his secrets could stay hidden for a while, maybe for tonight, or maybe for longer, who knew? He had to make peace with the idea he wasn't entirely honest. And maybe they could kiss. Not necessarily in that order.

And hopefully he could live with the deception.

CHAPTER TEN

Megan knew one thing: Cody Brennan had secrets. Things that he wasn't telling her anytime soon. Like whom he wrote lyrics for and what kind they were. What was his voice like, and how well could he dance, and why was he so evasive whenever she asked him about that. Cody didn't seem the kind to write for bands she'd never heard of. There was a vulnerability in him, sensitivity, compassion, and that was what she saw him writing. Love songs maybe, not words that had to be screamed over thrashing guitars. Then again, she didn't know him very well; under the smart guy sitting in front of her may well be the heart of a man who loved heavy metal and rock music.

Was that her fanciful way of thinking?

Seeing Kyle talking to him had been the jolt she needed. Hearing what her cousins and brother had to say about Cody coming from Kyle's mouth had made her more stubborn in the need to speak to this man and find out who he was.

She couldn't stop staring; he was strikingly handsome, sexy, with full lips, and a face made for the camera. Standing in front of her closet and deciding what to wear had been hard enough, she'd chosen jeans and the soft lavender shirt, casual, not expecting anything. But knowing how to act with this man now she was here was even worse. She was turned on by him, and that was a simple fact. From the hooded sweatshirt and beard when they first met to the formfitting shirt and jeans, he was sex on legs. And then add in the tattoos...

"What do they mean?" she asked, and touched the very edge of the tattoo she could see peeking from under his sleeve. He looked like he wanted to talk about everything but the tattoos; indecision was written in every line of his face.

"Those are stories for another time."

She nodded, respecting the words. Ink was a very personal thing. "Maybe on date four?" she asked. And that was probably the boldest she'd ever been. She waited for him to make excuses, but he didn't. He smiled. She didn't want to play games and seemed like he didn't either.

"Or the next one after that."

"You think there'll be at least five dates?"

Cody moved his fingers to rest on hers. "I hope so."

The touch of him was intoxicating, his hand warm, his gaze focused on her, wanting her, wanting to be with her, and she knew she'd let him.

"So tell me about your family, seeing as we've done mine."

"Mom and Dad are back in San Diego, where I grew up, and I have a sister and a nephew."

"Are you close?"

"We were," he said. "And we will be again. I'm just working up to contacting my sister. Thinking maybe she could come visit." He held up a hand to forestall her commenting, even though she hadn't been about to say anything. "Don't get me wrong, I want to be close to Emma, things got in the way. But she's on my list."

"List?"

"Of things I need to fix."

"You sound like you're at some kind of turning point in your life."

"I guess you could say that," he said.

She waited for more but he didn't offer anything. "What else is on the list?" she asked carefully.

Cody shrugged, but not dismissively, and he had an expression on his face that shouted confusion with a healthy mix of hope. "Lots of things, but the top of the list is kissing the beautiful woman opposite me."

He caught her gaze and waited for her to answer, or react, or whatever he expected from her. She hated this bit of dating, the trying to read the other person's mind, the part where you didn't quite know what to say. But then, she wanted to feel his lips on her too, so maybe she should be honest.

"We should go then," she said. She stood and Cody placed a pile of notes on the table. He hadn't asked for a check, and the money looked to be way more than was necessary, but she wasn't going to argue.

He thanked Kyle as they walked to the front of

the coffee shop, and shook his hand, complimented him on the meal, taking the easy smile he was given in return as some kind of tacit approval.

"I'll walk you home," he said when the door to the café closed behind them. The snow had stopped but the air was still icy cold and promised more snow as soon as everyone was in bed. Sure as anything they would all wake to a new blanket of frosty white.

"You won't have far," she said, disappointed, with a nod toward Notes & Roses. "Rachel and I live in the apartment over the shop."

He looked just as thwarted, and then his expression, lit by the soft glow of a streetlight, changed.

"Can we maybe, I mean, would you like to go for a walk then?" He pushed his hands into the pockets of his thick jacket. "Of course you wouldn't, way too cold."

The last thing Megan wanted was for this night to end. She held out her gloved hand and after a moment's hesitation Cody pulled his hand out of his jacket and took hold of hers.

"I'll show you the river," she said. She grasped hard and they crossed the main road. She hadn't held hands with a guy in a long time, but this felt entirely right. They made it to the small jetty behind the Stanford Creek Village Store. Less a shop for locals and more for visiting tourists, the soft lights inside illuminated the array of gifts and souvenirs, all showing the shape of the river in a stylized design.

"Do you know much about the town?" she asked.

"Not too much. I fell for the house and the state."

She dimpled a smile. "Easy to do. Well, we're in an oxbow of the Connecticut River," she explained. With her other hand she indicated the river to the left and right. "In the summer it's gorgeous, very sweet. Fast flowing so it doesn't tend to ice over, but the edges often collect ice." She toed at a spiky outcrop and it splintered and fell in the water. Small lights were entwined in the wooden rungs of the fencing that surrounded the jetty; the night was pitch black and a million stars were distant specks in the sky. This was the absolute perfect place for a kiss. God, she wanted to kiss him, to taste him, see if he was as good as she hoped in the fantasies she'd conjured in her head since he'd asked her out. He tugged her and she moved closer, and with his other hand he cradled her cheek and leaned in to kiss.

"Is this okay?" he asked softly, his words warm against her skin.

In answer she pushed herself up on her toes a little, gripped the front of his coat, and pressed her lips to his. The air was ice, their skin cold, but the kiss was all heat. She tilted her head, and the kiss deepened into a tangle of breath and taste. He moved his hands and widened his stance so he could tug her to slot between his thighs, and then closed his arms around her. In answer she laced her fingers behind his head, and they kissed again. How long they stood there in the cold, Megan couldn't begin to say, but she wasn't in a hurry to move, leaning against him, loving the warmth that built between them.

"I'd like to do that again," he murmured.

"Please." She didn't know if it was agreement or a plea for more, but he got with the program and soon the kisses were tinged with desperate need. The last kiss she'd had was with David, and that hadn't been a real kiss; in fact it had punctuated her whole understanding of who David was: controlled, domineering, icy cold. This kiss was fire and need and *God,* he tasted so good.

Lust shot through her as his hands slipped down to her ass and he lifted and tilted her. Not enough to press her close, he was giving her the chance to pull back. She didn't want space, she wanted herself right up against him, and she closed the final inch. He moaned into the press of her lips, and she felt so strong and certain in this. This was way more than a first kiss, this was erotic and hot and *more.*

She could feel him hard against her and if she moved a little more she could push herself there. She was already so close to losing her head from the kisses alone, God knew what it would be like if they were in bed. He released her slowly until her feet were flat on the floor, and he steadied her with a hand on her arm.

"Wow," he murmured, and brushed her lips with his bare fingers. "That was…"

"Yeah," she said with just as much coherence.

"We should…"

"Okay."

What he was saying, what she agreed to, she didn't know, swept away by the need to be back in his arms again. With unspoken agreement they left the jetty and walked back across the road and around the back of Notes & Roses to the stairs up to the small apartment. She knew Rachel was probably on the sofa with a book and would go to her room if Megan wanted her to, but somehow inviting Cody up didn't seem right. What they had was too unspoiled to be finished with meaningless sex.

"I don't know what to do next," she admitted. And that was a first. She always knew what she wanted to do.

Cody cradled her face again. "Part of me wants to come in, and kiss you some more, and hear you shout my name when I have you in my hands, but…"

Megan cleared her throat as finding words was suddenly very difficult. "But?"

"That's not how I want this to go, Megs. That would be the easy way, and I think this needs to be a special journey."

Disappointment warred with arousal. She could feel the touch of him, imagined him with his mouth on her, wanted him pushing inside her, and God, she swayed toward him.

"Don't," he warned in a soft tone. "Or I won't be the gentleman you need right now."

"Who says I need a gentleman?" she whispered.

Cody huffed a soft laugh. "It's what you deserve."

Megan stole one last kiss, knowing it had to be enough to see her through the night, and then stepped away.

"I think I hate you." She could feel herself pouting. Since when did she do that kind of thing?

Cody pressed a hand to his chest and pasted on a shocked expression. "You can't hate me, I'm made of awesome."

"I can't believe you just said that."

Cody smiled. "Get in, it's cold."

She climbed the stairs and let herself in, turning at the last moment to sketch a wave good-bye. He stood looking up at her and waved back, not moving an inch. She could call him up and do something about this intense need inside her. All she had to do was say the words.

Instead she shut the door and went straight through their small sitting room to her bedroom and locked herself in. She stripped for bed and removed her makeup, that delicious tension still in her body, sparking under her skin. Anticipation curled inside her as she climbed into bed, pressing against her heat, sighing as the intensity of those kisses came to the front of her mind. It took seconds, no more than that, until she was arching up into her hand, her whole body convulsing in orgasm.

It was with Cody's face in her thoughts, and his soft voice calling her 'Megs', that she slept.

"I want to know *all* the details," Rachel said for the third time. At least this time the question was accompanied by coffee, which Megan was nearly inhaling.

Despite a good night's sleep with Cody in her dreams, Megan wasn't up to handling Rachel's perky morning brightness. She perched on the stool behind the counter and sipped at her coffee.

"And?" Rachel demanded again. She'd begun with hinting at wanting to know everything, and then moved on to plain and simple questions. Part of Megan wanted to hoard selfishly all the emotions of the night before and not share at all, and that was a first. Megan and Rachel shared everything generally.

"And nothing," Megan replied, distracted. She concentrated on pricing up replacement flowers for Valentine's, in between sips of her now cooling coffee. She had to get in her order today to ensure she got everything she wanted. Valentine's was a busy time of the year, even in quiet Stanford Creek.

"Let me start, then. Garrett said Kyle talked to him and that he liked him."

That got Megan's attention and she looked up from the order. "Kyle liked him?"

"Garrett said, and I quote, he was all cute and flustered. Was he?"

"What?"

"Cute and flustered?"

Megan deliberately pushed the calculations to one side and picked up the second coffee Rachel had just collected from Carter's. Her cousin knew her so well that she'd need at least two before she was entirely coherent. Rachel was not going to stop asking, so she might as well get this over with. After all, it was what they did; after dates they dissected what happened. Only... this was different. But Rachel wouldn't know that, she'd expect the normal, the rating of one to ten, the chatting about the kissing, how far they'd gone, what he was like in bed.

"He left me at the door," Megan began. Not that she went to bed with men on the first date as a rule, but the slight disappointment in her tone would surely warn Rachel this was different.

Rachel placed her hands on her hips. "Hmm. Left at the door because there was no chemistry? Or left because there was too much?"

Megan looked at Rachel and raised a single eyebrow. "What do you think?"

"Oh wow, that good? When do you see him again?"

"I don't know. We didn't talk about that."

"Text him."

"I'm not a kid, I'm not texting him. Anyway, I don't have his number."

"You know where he lives. Go and find him, take him for a walk or coffee."

"I'm not walking up to his house—"

"Maybe I will then."

Megan stared at Rachel and watched for the smile that meant she was joking. There was no smile. "What?" They never went after each other's dates; that was a rule written when they'd both dated the same boy at age fourteen. They'd written it in the Megan and Rachel Book of Rules. Right alongside the rules about borrowing shoes and making sure to give them back.

Then Rachel's face split into a grin. "Joke."

Megan shook her head. "Bitch."

"Loser."

"Ho."

"Whatever."

The bell at the door sounded. A delivery man with a clipboard and a box under his arm strode in. "Can I get someone to sign for this?"

Rachel stepped forward, after all, it was her side of the business that accounted for most of the ad hoc deliveries. "This is for you," she said as she signed. Rachel placed the parcel on the counter before going back to her side of the shop and dealing with a customer who'd come in as the delivery guy left.

All Megan could think was that she hadn't ordered anything. She opened the box, pulling out the contents: two coffee table books, one of city views, the other of plants in a cottage garden. The invoice inside gave nothing away, more a packing slip than confirmation of who'd sent it.

She placed the books on the counter and went back to working on the bouquet someone had just called to order, a delicate mix of tiny roses. They weren't the kind of books she would buy for herself, but there was no doubting they were gorgeous, albeit probably very expensive gifts. She couldn't dispute they were for her, not with her name on the label and the dispatch note, but again with no note as to who they were from, she was confused.

This was either intriguing or slightly weird, but she hadn't decided which yet.

CHAPTER ELEVEN

Cody woke with a smile on his face and so much arousal flowing through him that even after getting himself off in the shower he was still half-hard. The images he had in his head of Megan under him, over him, coming apart under his hands were fuel to his already healthy imagination. He hadn't felt like this in a very long time. Today was a good day, a happy day, a day when he could walk into town and find out if Megan wanted lunch, or dinner. Or maybe they could just find a private space to stand and kiss. Kissing sounded pretty damn awesome right now.

He had two more missed calls from Danny, but not even that was going to faze him. He deleted the notes for them and clicked Google, searching for local stores that could make his living room look less empty.

Within ten minutes the cab he'd called was at his door. The man driving it—Harvey, Cody recalled—tipped an imaginary hat.

"Where to, Mr. Brennan?"

"Patterson Pianos, Montpelier, and then back."

"That's a hell of a run, gonna cost you."

"That's okay."

"Would be easier if you drove yourself." Harvey blinked innocently at him, and waited expectantly.

"I don't have a car," Cody answered. He kept the answer very simple; no point in going into details.

Instead of sitting in the back of the SUV, he chose to ride alongside Harvey. He had an underlying need to find out more about Megan, and Harvey could talk just as much as Eddie the barber. With some gentle prodding he hoped to learn everything Harvey knew about the family.

Of course, he couldn't come out and ask directly, that would guarantee Harvey would clam up tight. It seemed to Cody, Harvey was all about locals and family and history, but that maybe Cody hadn't entirely earned the trust to be told everything.

He did, however, find out a lot of interesting facts about how long the older families had been in Stanford Creek, starting with the Carters, who went back four generations. By the time they had driven the hour to Montpelier, Cody had learned a lot that filled in spaces, including the fact that there was a funding gap at the hospital and that the loss of Dr. Collins was a big thing, and would be significant to Megan, given her aunt would be left in the lurch.

He filed that one under bits of interesting news that he could use to get into Megan's good books. Although, to be fair, kissing had achieved that for both of them last night. They reached the piano shop and Harvey looked at him expectantly.

"How long you need?" He wasn't sure how long

it would take. He could take one look at the place and turn tail, go lick his wounds with a beer, or he could get into a conversation and be in there hours.

"Can I text you? I'll cover any expenses."

"Fifty dollars an hour," Harvey suggested. He narrowed his eyes as he said it.

"Deal."

They exchanged numbers and Cody watched as Harvey pulled away and into traffic. He'd enjoyed the journey over and hoped his good mood didn't fly away as soon as he tried to connect with music again. The shop itself was one of three wide-fronted businesses, sandwiched between a bridal place and a Mexican restaurant. The name, Patterson Pianos, Montpelier, was in gold lettering across the frosted glass, and the door had the sign turned to *Open*. It was stupid that a small part of him didn't phone ahead just so there was the off chance the place was shut. The sun was warm on his back, the snow cleared from the sidewalk, and the sky blue and empty of snow clouds.

"Coffee first," he said to no one, turning his back on the shop and spying a ubiquitous Starbucks on the opposite side of the road.

With a black coffee cooling in front of him he pulled out his cell and logged in to the free WiFi, locating the number he wanted and dialing it before he changed his mind.

"Notes & Roses, Megan speaking."

"Hey, it's me, Cody."

Silence. Was that a good thing? Should he add

some kind of description in case she didn't know who Cody was? Despite the date, he didn't want to assume anything. Then he heard some faint banging noises and Megan was back. "Hello?" She sounded like she was outside.

"Are you outside? Are you wearing a coat?" he asked immediately.

"Sorry?"

"You're outside?" For a second he thought he had blown it; after all, that was probably way too much worrying after one date. Right?

"Oh, that. Yes, I have a coat."

More silence.

"Thank you for last night," Cody said. And he meant it. He'd needed last night.

"I enjoyed it," Megan said. "All of it. I'd like to do it again."

"I realized I don't have your number, and I didn't give you mine. Like we didn't exchange or anything." He stopped himself before he talked himself in circles.

"You should come in and write it down for me." She'd lowered her tone, her voice dropping slightly, to something huskier and tinged with laughter, and he wasn't so rusty that he couldn't hear the flirting in it.

"Or I could pick you up and take you to dinner somewhere."

"I'd like that," she said, and he could hear a smile in her voice.

"Seven? Somewhere your family won't be able to find you."

"I'll be ready."

"Bye." Cody ended the call on that single word. Otherwise he could see it becoming one of those "you hang up" calls. He wasn't afraid to admit he was addicted to her voice; that much was clear. Finishing his coffee, buoyed by the fact he was seeing Megan later, he crossed back to the piano shop and stood outside. Then, with a conscious effort to calm the fuck down, he pushed the door open and stepped inside. The scents of polished wood and oil assaulted him and he inhaled it all.

"Good morning." A tall, slim woman stepped toward him. "Can I help?"

The woman stood between him and the pianos and stared at him with a friendly smile. The staring was unnerving; he should have gone when he still had the beard and the hair, been a little more Cody and a whole lot less CJ.

"I'd like to look around." He faltered when she pursed her lips. Maybe that wasn't how it was done? The piano he'd learned on at home had been there longer than he had, and the one he'd had in his house was brought in by management. He'd never browsed a piano shop with the actual money to buy. Ever.

"What is it you're looking for?" she asked.

"A Steinway, model S, baby grand. Do you have any?"

She looked him up and down and narrowed her eyes, like she was measuring him for size and fit and had found him lacking. She gestured to the nearest piano; not what he was looking for, but for some reason she wanted him to sit.

"Play me something," she said.

He stared at her, dumbfounded. Play her something? Now? In the middle of the day, in front of anyone who walked in? Looking around, he noticed two things. One, the shop was empty, and two, the acoustics with the low ceiling would be utter shit.

He was rusty. His fingers ached to connect with the keys, his back straightening as he sat on the stool and assessed the piano. Nothing came to mind and he depressed a chord, the tone of it enough to have him smile. He closed his eyes and attempted to forget he had an audience, albeit of only one, playing a few moments of the first song he could think of, one by Hudson Hart, a soft romantic ballad, before opening his eyes.

A broad grin split her face. "This way," she said, visibly vibrating with enthusiasm. "Derek, my husband that is, says we need to be more circumspect in whom we allow to see our pianos, but I have a good feel for you, young man."

"You do?" Cody followed her through the main showroom and past a small desk covered with papers.

"What is your budget?"

"I, uhm… don't have one."

"We have some easy payment terms with a deposit, can you manage a deposit?"

"I'll pay for the whole thing now," he said. His admission was hard. Would she look at him differently if she knew he could drop the entire forty thousand needed to buy the piano he wanted? Maybe more than that?

She nodded, like she knew something, almost as if she knew who he was, or suspected, and it made him feel a little sick with nerves. Then, she opened a final door with a flourish, and all his nerves were gone. There it was, the wood polished to a high sheen, the most beautiful thing he'd seen, in a high-ceilinged room.

And he knew one thing. It was his.

She left him after a few minutes and he sat and played, time almost slowing to nothing as he lost himself in the notes. She came back to check on him, and he didn't hesitate. He paid in full, delivery was agreed upon, and abruptly he was back outside the shop. Texting Harvey, he waited by the coffee shop, staring at Patterson's Pianos and contemplating one hell of a lot of things.

Mostly, though, he thought that maybe, with a piano in the house, he could find some words to go along with the music.

And he couldn't wait to show Megan.

"Can we find a deli somewhere?" he asked as he climbed into the car. He wasn't an amazing cook, but he could throw together pasta and sauce and add in some deli bits and pieces, olives and cheese on the side. *Maybe I should get candles?* Would she hate it if he took her to his house? Would it be a step too far, too fast? He didn't have a car, should he book Harvey to take them to Coleville? That was the nearest town with restaurants in which the rest of Megan's family would be far enough away not to pop up mid-date. Not that it worried him, but Megan seemed tired of it.

But then Harvey would know. And he could promise Megan right off the bat that this was a platonic getting-to-know-you date.

I'll ask, and if she seems worried, I'll call Harvey.

Deep inside, in the dark scary parts of him, he knew he needed to get back behind the wheel of a car. He had three of them, all lined up in his six-car garage under the house back in San Diego. Once, he'd loved cars, collected them as a hobby, old cars he polished and loved. But that had been then. Things had changed.

They stopped at the deli and Cody picked up what he needed, along with extras like wine and flavored waters and Sprite, not knowing what she liked to drink.

When he got home he attempted to make the place look a little more lived in. He'd bought some crockery, nice stuff, not the bargain stuff he'd gotten on his way here, and napkins, and even some cutlery that looked sturdy and bright when he ran a cloth over it to shine it up. He felt positively domesticated until he turned to survey what he'd done, and wished his place didn't look so bland. He hadn't put his mark on it, and considered asking Zee to send over some of the things he had at home. Although that would have to be for next time.

When his alarm told him it was six-thirty, he surveyed his dining room. There was no table as such, but there was a huge sofa and a small coffee table, and stools that pulled up to a breakfast bar in the kitchen. He lowered the lights a little, placed candles to one side for later, and then, seeing he could do no more, he locked up the house and walked down the hill to Main. He was early so he bypassed the road to walk through the park, following the pathways that were still visible as indentations in the deeper snow. He was treading in the new stuff, freshly fallen, although there was no snow tonight.

The snow made the town beautiful, more beautiful than it was already. There was something about snow and the way it cloaked even the bad parts.

More lyrics came into his head, and this time when he deliberately thought about something else, they were still there.

Finally, something was sticking.

CHAPTER TWELVE

Cody finally made it to the back entrance of Megan and Rachel's apartment a little before seven. He didn't have to climb the steps, Megan was waiting at the bottom, just to one side, in the shadows, and she looked at him expectantly.

They walked toward each other, meeting in the middle and, as they met, her hands clasped around the back of his neck, his hands holding her weight, and they kissed like they'd never kissed before. She moaned into the kiss and he stepped her backward until her butt hit the iron of the banister. She huffed into the kiss as he pressed against her and that small sound was enough to have him pulling back, gently untangling her hands from behind his head.

"Hey," he said.

"Hey yourself."

"I've wanted to do that all day."

"Me too."

They kissed again, this time a lighter touch, a hello framed with smiles. Then, with her hand tucked into the crook of his arm, they walked from the apartment and the shops.

"I have something to ask you," Cody said as they walked past the front of Notes & Roses. "I thought we could eat at my house; it's private, and I promise you nothing will happen, just eating and talking."

Megan stopped the walk and pulled him to a stop. "Hang on," she said, and fumbled with her cell. After some typing she pocketed it again. "I need to tell Rachel where I am, who I'm with. Safety things."

"You take safety seriously," Cody said, for conversation, as they began to make their way up the hill.

"I have two scary brothers; the horror stories I got told growing up were horrible."

"It's good that they look out for you. My sister is too far away for me to do that."

They moved to one side of the path to make way for an older man being taken for a walk by his huge bear of a dog.

"Evening, Megan," the man said.

"Hi, Mr. Sooner. Hi, Bear," she replied. She stooped and made a fuss of the dog, some kind of a mountain lion and poodle mix with curiously curly fur, and there wasn't any more conversation as the aptly named Bear dragged his owner toward the park.

"You like dogs?" Cody asked. He wanted to know everything about her, from whether she loved animals to whether she liked former boy band singers. Of course, he was working his way up to that last revealing series of questions.

"I love dogs. Mom and Dad used to have dogs all the time when we all lived at home. But when it was just them, they never replaced Sasha when she passed, she was a black lab, fifteen you know."

"Wow, that's a good age. So you don't want a dog of your own now?"

"Rachel and I share a poky apartment, and we're working a lot. I can't see it happening yet. Maybe in a couple years."

She shivered as a gust of icy wind circled them, and snuggled into him closer, and he felt like the tallest man in the world. They hurried their steps a little and made it to the blue house quickly.

"Careful, the wood is treacherous," he cautioned as they climbed the steps to the front of the wraparound porch. "I've put salt on it, and tried to get as much ice off as I could."

"This is where you fell?" She was curious and stared down at the ground as if she was looking for something to blame.

"Yeah." He fumbled with his key to open the door and pushed it open with a flourish, encouraging her in and closing the door behind them as quick as possible. They stripped off coats and boots and he turned to her to ask if it was okay for them to eat in the kitchen, given he didn't have much furniture. The words stopped in his throat as he saw her staring into the main front room with a sad expression on her face.

"I remember this place so well," she half-whispered. "So many memories."

"Is everything okay? I'm sorry, are the memories too much?" It was on the tip of his tongue to suggest that he call a real estate agent and move. He should have thought this through a lot more; she'd known the young guy who'd died.

"Not at all. Matt was always going to be in the army, from when I first met him. I was five and he was in my class, and from that first day he told us he was going to be a soldier."

She still looked pensive and he grasped her hand. "I want to show you something, though you've probably already seen it." He led her to the empty dining room that in daylight hours had a view of the river, and stopped at the doorjamb. She peered at the marks, a fond smile on her face.

"Jamie always was taller, but Matt was broad. Last time I saw Matt he was in uniform, looking very handsome."

"The barber, I forget his name?"

"Eddie."

"Yeah, he said that Matt was a hero. I mean, all soldiers are heroes in my mind, but he seemed to be alluding to something specific."

Megan traced the marks in the wood. "Matt saved two of his teammates under heavy fire. I remember how proud his mom and dad were." She looked up at him. "Will you renovate this place?"

Cody blinked at the sudden change in direction of the conversation. He glanced around at the solid wood, at the sturdy walls, and shook his head. "I like it as it is."

"If you do, if you ever feel like you want to leave, do you think you could somehow…" She tapped the wood with the marks. "I think Jim and Barbara would regret their decision not to have this."

"Of course."

They stood there a little longer, Cody realizing that Megan needed some time to process what she was doing in the house, to have some time with her memories. "I'll be in the kitchen," he murmured. She looked at him and nodded.

"I'll be there in a few seconds."

He made himself busy in the kitchen, lighting the candles on the breakfast bar and dimming the lights. Pasta sauce on the warmer and water bubbling away ready for the pasta, he opened the wine and considered what the etiquette was on red wine and whether he should have opened it earlier.

"That looks kind of fancy," Megan teased. She picked up the bottle and checked the label after he poured her a generous glass. "Do you know wine?"

"No. I guess I should have asked if you even wanted wine."

"Wine, chocolate, no need to check with me first." She sipped at the red and the tip of her tongue darted out to taste the wine on her lips.

Instant arousal. It seemed in Cody's case it was just add wine and Megan, and he was turned on. He cupped her face and kissed the spot where the wine had lingered, and the kiss deepened for a little while, stopped only by the alarm on the stove telling him the pasta was done. Reluctantly they pulled apart and Cody decided now would be a good time to tell Megan a small truth.

"I've never kissed anyone as much as I've kissed you in the last two days. I can't get enough of you," he said bluntly. Then before she could answer he turned away to deal with dinner, and she didn't immediately reply.

He'd probably fucked up admitting such a thing on the second date, but hell, he had to have at least one truth out there.

"I like kissing you too," she said, with a lot more finesse than he'd used. Shyness stole over him, and he realized his life had become so fucked up that he'd lost the ability to express how he was feeling. No management on tour was interested in how he felt, only how much they could get from him.

Screwed, totally screwed in the head.

Then the rational side of him pushed the pity to one side. *People would kill for the chances you had.* He concentrated on draining the pasta, leaving a little of the water and then pouring in the tomato, garlic, and chili sauce. Finally he served a plate of hot pasta to a smiling Megan. It looked a little messy, he wasn't adept at serving the slippery spaghetti and sauce for guests. Generally he ate it in a big bowl and it didn't matter how messy he got. This was different, but still, he felt he should say something.

"Guess I should have done something a little less messy," he admitted and frowned down at his plate.

Megan inhaled deeply. "Smells wonderful."

She did this twisting thing with the fork and

spoon and, with practiced ease, took her first mouthful of the tomato and pasta, closing her eyes and savoring the taste.

"Nice," she announced, "just like Mom would make." She winked at him and he immediately thought two things, one, that she was probably teasing him, and two, that she looked damn cute when she winked.

Cody attempted to get a forkful to his mouth, finally giving up and chopping the pasta into small pieces instead. He tasted it, and yes, it was good. He felt pride that he'd managed to make something edible and thanked the heavens his mom had shown him how to cook a few meals for when he went on the road. She was the typical mom from storybooks, always cooking and baking and generally feeding up the family. But even she had seen that a man needed to be able to make spaghetti. He recalled she'd apologized when she was showing him, muttering that a better mom would have taught her son how to bake and cook a lot earlier than she had. All he'd said back was that he would never have listened, that music was his soul. She'd laughed and said he'd starve. *Fond memories of a time before Hudson Hart.*

"Do you like cooking?" she asked after taking a sip of the wine, interrupting the memories.

"I can cook tomato pasta," he said. "And microwave things; I'm an expert at nuking things."

They finished eating and, with wine in hand, they moved to the sofa. He didn't want to read anything into the fact that Megan sat right at the other end of the wide seating. She curled her legs up and half turned to face him, and she was smiling.

Okay, so this was how it worked in the real world. He'd gone from teenage dates that were all about getting off as fast as you could, to having women on call if he wanted them. With nothing in between.

Centering himself and sipping heady red wine, he decided he liked this new learning experience.

They talked for a long time and, at some point not long after midnight, they decided it was a good idea for Megan to get home. Bundled in coats, holding hands, they walked down the hill and the natural conversation continued. Megan loved big ballad singers, he admitted to his love of all things Rat Pack, she countered that she loved Frank Sinatra and it reminded her of what her granddad loved to listen to. Which led to Cody pouting and Megan laughing, and kissing the pout away.

And right there and then, a small part of Cody's heart was lost to Megan.

Completely and irretrievably lost.

CHAPTER THIRTEEN

Megan woke with a smile on her face at the memories of the previous night. Everything had been so easy; the talking, the kissing, the entire time she'd spent with Cody had her smiling like an idiot now.

The smile followed her to work and, despite two minor catastrophes, was still on her face at lunchtime. So much so that Rachel would not leave her alone. She wanted to know every detail and, selfishly, Megan wanted to hoard everything to herself.

The first catastrophe was that the delivery van they used had two flat tires. Not just one, but two.

"You must have driven over something sharp," Rachel commented as the two of them, in their thick coats, crouched down by the tires both with holes in them. "Something under the snow."

Megan kicked one of the flat tires. "Stupid thing."

But that hadn't been enough to clear her smile.

The second had sorely tested her, when she went to put the A-Board outside the shop, promoting Valentine's, and slid on her ass down the single step. Rachel came out after her yelp of surprise and helped her stand.

"You okay?"

Megan rubbed her ass and winced. "I'm okay, jeez, that step."

"I'm sure I salted it when I first got here, along with the sidewalk where it's iced up," Rachel said with a frown. She poked at the step and grimaced. "It's a sheet of ice." She reached up and over the step and came back with more salt, scraping away the ice with Megan's assistance, and making sure there was enough salt on there to melt a glacier. "I'm sorry, Megs, I must have forgotten part of it."

Megan side hugged Rachel. "These things happen," she said as philosophically as she could when her ass hurt.

And now it was lunchtime, and still the smile remained.

"So you kissed," Rachel said. Again. She'd not believed Megan any of the times Megan had said it.

"Yes, we kissed, and yes, he walked me home." Megan sent her cousin a look that she hoped spoke volumes, and went back to the display she was working on. The bell sounded and she looked up, her chest tightening when she thought it could be Cody, disappointed when she saw it was David.

The evil part of her she kept well-hidden was disappointed that it hadn't been David who'd fallen on his ass on the step.

"Can I help you?" Rachel moved between David and Megan, and Megan was never more thankful for having a little spiky pit bull for a cousin.

"I'm here to talk to Megan," David said. He

attempted to sidestep Rachel but she was having none of it and managed to herd him back to the door.

"She doesn't want to see you," Rachel said firmly.

"Five minutes." David darted left and managed to bypass Rachel, striding quickly to the counter. "I want to order some flowers."

Rachel was at his side a millisecond later, but Megan gave a small shake of her head. *He's not worth it,* she attempted to telegraph through that motion alone. Rachel got the hint and moved away, but only as far as the nearest notebook selection.

"What kind of flowers?" Megan asked in her most professional voice. He looked a little glassy-eyed, and she considered he might well have been drinking.

"A large bouquet. A thank-you." He spoke in the very deliberate tone used by drunks, so she was probably right about the alcohol.

Megan pulled her notebook close to her. "Budget?"

"No budget, I want it to be beautiful like you."

Megan groaned inwardly. Would this man not get the hint?

"David, stop, okay? That was a serious question."

He leaned on the counter and used his best soulful expression. "I was being serious, I've never seen anything as beautiful as you."

This was going beyond annoying and on to creepy. She'd told him no, let him down as softly as she could, but he wasn't getting the point. She dropped her pen and pushed the notepad to one side.

"I'd like you to leave."

"Megan, the flowers would be for you, like the roses I sent."

"The roses were from you?"

"You remind me of a rose."

Behind him Rachel made a gagging motion, and Megan had to try hard not to join in.

"You. Need. To. Leave."

Desperation lit in David's eyes. "Megan. Did you like the books? They were beautiful, right? And the real estate agent said he'd get good money for the place; there's no reason why you couldn't leave and come with me as my wife."

"What the hell?" Megan's stomach gave a sickening lurch.

"And you don't need Rachel, she already forgot to clear the step and made you fall."

"Right here!" Rachel reminded him loudly.

There was way too much information to process in David's rambling announcements. "I will call Justin," Megan repeated. "Now."

"I said I want some flowers—"

"There's a grocery store; you can get some there."

"But I want them delivered," he protested.

"No deliveries, the van is out of commission today."

"Yes, I heard." He leered at her, calculation in his gaze. "Shame about the tires."

Megan didn't recall mentioning the tires to anyone but the garage, and her chest tightened.

Abruptly David was slipping into psycho territory. And, he was still talking.

"Maybe you should give up on deliveries. In New York you wouldn't need a van, everything is so close, and I would be okay with you having some kind of small investment in a shop. Maybe you could go in a few hours a day."

Megan had no words at first, and then she knew exactly what she wanted to say. "Out of my shop."

"Megan, you're being ridiculous. Listen to me; we'd be perfect for each other."

"Leave. Now."

The bell sounded again, and this time when she glanced over and saw it was Cody she immediately wanted to disappear. What would he think about David and his words and the flattering and the fact that he wouldn't leave the shop? She looked like an idiot even allowing David face time like this. *I should have called Justin.* In fact, she'd gone past annoyed and was moving straight to uncomfortable to have David in the shop like this. His fake affection was spinning into sneering.

David leaned even further over the counter, into her space, and gone was the desperation; now he was smirking, his eyes assessing. He'd evidently decided romance wasn't cutting it and now he was going down that weird-ass cajoling path he inevitably used.

"Megs, come on… We can be good together." He sounded a little desperate.

"Go away, David. Just, please leave me alone."

She sensed Cody coming toward them, and

Megan was torn between poking David in the eye with a pen and wishing the world would open up and swallow him.

Then her world really did shift. Cody bypassed the counter, walked around the back of it, pulled her close, and kissed her thoroughly. She swore that a squeak left her mouth, but she couldn't help melting a little into the kiss. Jeez, Cody was good at kissing. They separated, and Cody, all smooth and like he wasn't aware David was there all through the kiss, held out a hand to the other man.

"Hey, Cody Brennan," he began. "We met in the hospital, Dr....?"

"Collins," David bit out. He released the shake and backed away from them. Then he looked directly at Megan. "I can't believe this. How could you, after..." He ran out of words and with a scowl he stormed out of the shop and slammed the door shut behind him. Megan watched him leave, heard Rachel's snort of laughter as he slid a little on the sidewalk, looked around to check if anyone had seen, and then continued on up the road in the direction of the hospital.

"Asshole," Cody muttered.

Megan shoved him in the chest. "He's the asshole? What did you just do?"

Cody opened and closed his mouth a couple times, then the puffed-up manly thing he had going on subsided to a somewhat sheepish expression. "Uh-oh," he said.

She poked him in his chest, stopping herself from

flattening her hand and sliding her palm over the muscles.

"Yeah, uh-oh is right."

"What can I do to make it better?" he asked, looking away from her briefly. She could see the twitch of his mouth; the bastard was going to laugh at her.

This time she slapped his chest with the flat of her hand. She wasn't going to admit that what he'd done had, first of all, been incredibly hot, and secondly, would stop David in his tracks. Nope, she was angry, dammit.

"You're worse than my brothers."

A wounded look passed over his face. "That hurts," he said. Then he pulled her in roughly for another kiss and her body didn't go on an automatic overload shutdown. When he released his hold there was a faint ripple of applause and Megan turned to see Rachel clapping, Justin frowning with arms crossed over his chest, Kyle grinning like an idiot, and Garrett with hands in his pockets looking broody.

"Rachel?"

"I 911'd, and I'm not sorry I did," she admitted. "David was smarming you."

"That's not even a word," Megan was keen to point out.

"Anyway," Rachel said cheerfully. "We didn't need any of them." She indicated the three men ranged around her.

"Seems like she has someone to protect her now," Kyle said. He winked at Megan and was the first to leave. Justin didn't move, Garrett either.

"We need to talk," Justin said.

"I don't need to talk," Megan snapped.

"I didn't mean I needed to speak to *you*." He looked pointedly at Cody.

Megan stiffened, walked to Justin, and shoved him toward the door, then did the same with Garrett; she opened the door and held it open deliberately.

"I love you both, but I've had a shit morning and I want you to go away, okay?"

They muttered something between them but stepped outside the shop. Which left Cody, who looked way too smug not to have been ordered out.

"Go," she said.

"Me?"

"You. Out as well."

Cody reached the door, but at the last minute he stopped and kissed her. Not hard, not thoroughly, just a simple kiss good-bye. "See you later."

And then he, too, was gone.

She turned on her heel to speak to Rachel, who was grinning. "Like your style," she said and held up her palm to high five. Megan ignored her.

She couldn't keep the shock out of her voice. "You 911'd them all?"

"Before Cody got here, yes. I don't like David."

"I can't believe he said all that shit."

"You think he cut the tires on the car?"

"You picked that up as well?"

"Yep. What about the ice on the steps? What if he poured water on them after I salted, and it washed away, and iced over?"

"That's a reach, even for David."

"So you do think he slashed the tires."

Megan shook her head tiredly. "I don't know. No, he couldn't have. He's an idiot, but he's not a criminal."

"I'm not sure he's right in the head," Rachel added. "I saw his face when Cody was kissing you; if he'd had a weapon, Cody would be dead."

"Shit, Rachel, that's a little dramatic." Megan couldn't conceive of something like that happening. It didn't bear thinking about.

"I know. Let's talk about what Cody did."

"Let's not."

"That was hot. Really hot."

Megan deflated. She couldn't lie to Rachel; it had been hot, Cody coming to her aid and staking his claim, and she'd allowed it to happen.

So much for the strong confident single woman who could handle anything.

"Admit it," Rachel teased. "That was hot."

Megan rolled her eyes, then leaned back on the counter and made a show of fanning herself with the notebook. "So hot."

"That man can kiss."

"God yes."

And that was how they spent the next hour dissecting kissing techniques all the way back to Simon in the third grade who had kissed Rachel, and then Megan, as a dare.

And through all of it, Megan was on edge. She laughed and reminisced as she worked, but she had to admit David's visit had been unnerving, unsettling, and that Cody's assumption that he could near brand her in public was at the same time hot and infuriating.

Only when Rachel left for the coffee run and Megan was alone in the shop did she take the time to breathe and admit to her single strong self that yep, Cody was an equally strong man who knew which of her buttons to push.

And boy, was she enjoying it.

She needed to get back at him somehow, put things back on the same level, show him he wasn't in charge of her, that she could rock his world as easily as he seemed to rock hers.

And she knew exactly how she was going to do it.

Cody opened the door and moved sideways to let her in, watching as she stripped off her jacket and looked cautious. She wasn't angry as such, more focused on what needed to be done.

"Let's sit," she said, and walked into the front room. He followed her and she rounded on him.

"I'm in trouble, aren't I?" he said. "I want to apologize but I didn't like—" He let out a loud oomph as she pushed him and he toppled backward onto the sofa. In an instant, using his surprise to her advantage, she straddled him and settled into his lap.

"Don't do it again," she murmured, before kissing him. He attempted to deepen the kiss, his hands curving around her ass and shuffling her closer. She pulled away and he chased for the kiss. She wasn't ready to be kissing, she had things she had to say.

"You think you can be all hero tough guy, all alpha, and I'm telling you I already have three of those in my life, so while I get what you did, and it was freaking hot—"

"It was?" he interrupted, brightening considerably.

"Shut up," she ordered. "Do it again and I will knee you where it hurts."

He opened his mouth to talk, and she swallowed any words he may have had in a heated kiss, all the while shifting on his lap, and gripping his shoulders tight. He was so hard under her, his arms strong, his hold on her ass steady and firm.

"I want my hands on you," he whispered between kisses.

"Not yet," she said, and then, before he could say another thing, she escaped his hold and stood up. He looked up at her, blinking and surprised at the sudden loss.

"What's wrong?"

"You came into my shop, kissed me, and left me so turned on I couldn't think for the rest of the afternoon."

He winced. "Should I take that as a compliment?"

"Take it any way you like it, but I'm going now."

He palmed his erection and wriggled a little. "Going?" He looked like the bottom had fallen out of his world.

"Then you'll know what it's like to be left all

turned on with no action after," she continued. Her resolve was weakening and any minute now she'd let out the laugh she'd been trying to keep in at his crestfallen expression. His handsome face was creased into a frown that was adorable. "Have you learned your lesson?" she said, and the laugh left her in a snort.

His dejected look morphed into suspicion and he narrowed his eyes at her. "Why are you laughing?"

In a smooth move she straddled him again. "You're lucky I'm only leaving you turned on for a few minutes."

He got with the plan very quickly. "So we're even; can I touch you now?"

They laughed as he attempted to get her top off as she fiddled with the heavy belt of his jeans. Only when she was down to her bra on top, and he was only covered with his boxers, did they stop laughing and teasing.

She moved a little against him and he groaned and captured her covered breasts in his hands. He weighed them, curved the shape of them, and ran his thumbs over her nipples, sending lightning to the very center of her. She moaned into the touch, and ground down a little, swallowing his answering curse in a kiss. He encouraged her to lean back, sucking gently on her nipples, pressing his fingers into the skin at her hip bone. Even like this, with material between them, Megan burned, orgasm building inside her, sparking and washing from where they slotted together to his hands, and he knew it.

"So close," he said as he stared into her eyes with his intense brown gaze. "Come on, I want to see you go over." He slid her over him, his erection pressing in all the right places. She needed more, needed his hands on her breasts, and he seemed to know. Pushing aside her bra, he took first one nipple into his mouth then moved to the other, all while he rocked her against him. They kissed and rutted and she was turned on to the point he could probably suggest they make love and she wouldn't say no. The thought of him being inside her was enough that she couldn't think or breathe. Sensation flooded her, pushing her over until she arched into his hold and pressed herself hard against him.

He caught her moan of completion in a heated kiss, pushing up against her and groaning his own release as she lay limp against him.

They lay breathing heavily, wrapped in each other's arms.

"God," he whispered against her heated skin. "What you do to me."

All she did was snuggle into his hold.

Right then, at that moment, she was the strongest woman alive.

CHAPTER FOURTEEN

"Are you falling asleep?" Cody asked. He used his gentlest tone, part of him hoping she was falling asleep on him just so he had an excuse to sit there and hold her for the rest of the evening. She smelled so good, apples and snow and all things in between, and he wanted more of that. Of course, it would be nice if he could get up and change his underwear at some point, but he'd put up with any discomfort just to be here.

"No," she murmured. But to make her words a lie, she snuggled in deeper and yawned.

"Are you okay?"

"Uh-huh."

Evidently coherency was gone, and he chuckled. "We should get a blanket and never move."

"Ever?"

"Never."

"What about food?" She lifted her head from his chest and looked at him a little sadly.

"You're right, we'd fade away and die, but we'd be warm and together."

She scooted away from him a little and then

eased herself off, falling in a heap to one side then staring up at the ceiling. "I probably need food."

Did she know what she looked like? All limp and spread-eagled on his sofa, her lips swollen with kisses, and her eyes heavy lidded. He'd never seen anything so perfectly beautiful, or so damn sexy.

A cell sounded before he could speak and suggest she stayed the night. She reached for the purse she'd discarded and dug out the phone, peering at the screen and connecting the call.

"Joe, hey... okay..." Her expression changed quickly from fondness to resignation, and back to fondness again. "I'll come by in the morning." She ended the call with a good-bye and tossed her cell toward her purse. "Well, that's about right," she said dramatically.

"What?" Cody scooted up and fastened his jeans, leaving his belt unbuckled.

"Joe, he's the mechanic who looks after the cars in town, has a place on Chapel Road."

"I don't think I know him."

"He's a good guy but even he can't fix the stupid in me. Another bill for tires."

It was on the tip of Cody's tongue to help somehow, but now was the time to be supportive. "Sorry."

"It's okay." She sighed and sat up. "My creepy ex is sending me flowers, and I hope I drove over something in the snow, two tires slashed on the car."

"You hope? That's an odd thing to say."

"Rachel is convinced he did it, but I have to believe it was me."

Cody's chest tightened both at the mention of the ex, and the single word slashed. Megan rolled up off the sofa, rearranged her bra, and slipped her top back on. Cody was way too concerned about her use of the word *slashed* to even think of commenting on how he didn't want her to cover up.

Has to be an accident, it can't be deliberate.

"Never mind, ignore me, it's been a weird week, expensive too."

"Should you talk to your brother?"

"Rachel told him everything David said, and Justin said he'd keep an eye on things. But, David is a doctor, for God's sake. He's a man with a career, a fancy job in New York, and lots of money. He could have any woman he wanted, why would he fixate on me?"

Cody knew how she was feeling. Julia was a sound engineer, one of the guys almost, a woman with a purpose in her life. But she'd turned and become something evil. Now wasn't the time to pull that shitfest into the conversation.

"Sorry," he said, lamely.

"Meh, these things happen." She patted her stomach and held out a hand, which he took to stand up. "I'm hungry. Feed me."

Cody put aside misgivings, and that instant of fear that had gripped him when he recalled awful memories. Pushed to the edge, he'd only felt partially safe when his stalker ended up behind bars. Just because Megan had used the word slashed didn't mean the tires had been knifed as his had been. And they'd found no evidence linking his stalker to the tires, but Cody just *knew* it was her.

Instead he focused on grabbing anything in the fridge that was edible, and with plates of bits and pieces they opened a new bottle of red and lost a whole evening to talking and kissing.

And not once did he mention a stalker, nor anything that would take them in a circular way to the person he really was.

But instead of feeling calm and in charge, he felt guilty. Wouldn't hurt to visit Sheriff Campbell and make sure the tire issue was an accident, and maybe mention what had happened to him. The anxiety and guilt and every other fucked-up emotion inside him twisted and churned together until he was suddenly sick with fear.

"Are you okay?"

He could trust Megan, she wasn't going to run out on him, or ask him for things he wasn't ready to give. He even formulated how to start the conversation, had the whole first sentence in his head.

Instead, he held her in a tight hug and suggested they go back to hers before it was too late. If she saw it as a dismissal she didn't say anything, and they held hands as they walked back to Megan's place.

By the time they reached the iron steps to her apartment, Cody had settled his mind. Counseling had gotten him so far, but his own strength to compartmentalize things was how he managed life.

"You want to come in for coffee?" she asked as they hugged at the bottom of the stairs.

"Not this time," he said, and kissed her good night. He'd just about got his head around the small panic attack tonight; he was ready for some space now to work on what he was thinking.

It didn't seem like she had a problem, waved at him from the door, and then closed it. For a while Cody stood where he was, scuffing patterns in the snow at the base of the stairs.

"You waiting until she goes to sleep?"

He recognized the voice. The middle sibling, Garrett. He turned to face him.

"No," Cody said. "Just thinking."

"What about?" Garrett wasn't moving, had his feet planted firmly in the snow, his hands in his pockets, and his expression intense under the soft glow of the outside light attached to the wall.

"Things."

Garrett nodded, and Cody walked past him and down Main, leaving the unsettling man behind.

The first thing he did when he got home was to phone Zee, ignoring her grumbling about only phoning when he wanted something.

"Is Ortiz still behind bars?" he asked without explanation.

"Why? What's wrong?"

"Can you find out for me?"

"She's not due out for a long time, Cody."

"What if she gets out on a psych evaluation, or a good behavior bond or something?"

"Cody, she murdered Leah."

"Find out for me. As soon as you can."

"Wait, you sound weird. Has something happened?"

Well? Had something happened? Was it the tire thing, and the fact he always suspected Julia Ortiz had slashed his tires? Or was it that he was getting too close to Megan and abruptly had something precious in his life to lose? "Not really, I was just thinking," he lied.

"Go to bed, Cody, it must be midnight where you are. Oh, and have you called Danny? He tried your number, said it went directly to voicemail."

"Good night, Zee," Cody responded, and ended the call as abruptly as he had made it.

He'd seen the messages, not listened to them, but seen them. Four in all. He should probably delete them otherwise the box would fill and if someone important tried to get hold of him...

Who was he kidding? Danny had been one of the most important parts of his life for such a long time, yet he couldn't even think of listening to his voice? Was it because it linked to Hudson Hart and dredged up way too much crap in his head?

This was getting fucking ridiculous.

Deliberately he placed the phone on the small coffee table, turned the volume up and pressed Play on the message screen, forcing it to the loudspeaker.

The first message was so simple. *Hey, it's me, Danny. Can you phone me back, buddy? Thanks... bye.*

The second was similar, stating he wasn't sure Cody got his first message, only the tone of the voice was more focused and the last bit a plea that made Cody cringe. *Please, CJ, I really need to talk to you.*

He paused the playback and recalled the last time he'd spoken face-to-face with his best friend. At the restaurant in LA; he'd told Danny what had happened between him and Katya, and Danny had punched him so hard he'd ended up on his back in the middle of forty diners.

And there it was: Katya, the thorn in his side, Danny's girlfriend and then fiancée, a gold-digging bitch who'd promised Danny the earth, pretended love, and then climbed into Cody's bed as soon as Danny's back was turned.

Cody had thrown her out, told his friend, and Danny had turned on him.

And *now* he wanted back in Cody's life, and what was stopping Cody? They'd had misunderstandings before, arguments over music, over money, hell, over Cody's bike that Danny had trashed when they were only eleven. They'd sung together, played hard together, and through it all Cody had Danny as his wingman.

All gone because of a stalker and a girlfriend.

He pressed *Play.*

CJ, I don't know if you are listening to these messages, or if you are deleting them as they come in. I wish you'd pick up the phone and talk to me, because I need to hear your voice. There's something you should know, something I need help with. Quiet, Danny obviously needed to think about what he was saying next. *Fuck, CJ, please call me. Please, man.*

The fourth message had a lot of static at the start, and he couldn't make out the beginning, but the rest of it was clear.

...I don't know who else to turn to, I'm so sorry for everything, I want you to know that and whatever happens... Cody, whatever I have to do... I love you, brother.

That was it. All four messages played, and only when he heard Danny call him by his real name, not the fake stage persona that was CJ, did the emotion inside him break free. He bowed his head as anger at himself curled inside him. They'd been as close as brothers could be, and family found a way through the mess of life.

Would it hurt to see what Danny wanted? Just because they talked didn't mean Cody needed to be dragged back into Hudson Hart. He picked up the cell and clicked *Reply* before he could second-guess himself, his chest tightening as he waited for it to connect. Danny answered nearly immediately.

"CJ?" he asked, his tone shocked.

"Cody," Cody corrected him automatically. He'd spent so long doing that with Zee that it was second nature.

"Okay." Danny sounded uncertain. "I didn't expect... You dropped the CJ thing then."

Cody could remember the day they decided Cody was too pedestrian a name and that CJ was cooler. They'd both not long turned seven, and had a heated debate over whether Danny could use his middle name of Ewan to be known as DE.

"DE doesn't work," Cody had insisted.

"I want a cool name too."

Cody had punched him in the arm. "Danny is already a cool name, idiot."

And now this was them talking, and a great icy wall existed between them.

"What do you want?" Cody asked. He couldn't help the resignation in his voice. The one person he'd always thought would have his back had vanished as soon as the shit hit the fan. Talking to Danny was a mistake and he almost cut the call, only Danny spoke, and his voice was so low and broken that it sent shivers down Cody's spine.

"I need help, Cody. And you're the first person, the only person, I want to talk to."

"Well, you must have spoken to Zee for her to tell me you'd called." This wasn't him. He wasn't a pedantic kind of person. He knew he was being hard, and childish even, and he attempted to rein it in.

"Zee was just there to help me get to you. Jeez, Cody, it's good to hear your voice."

"Help how?" Cody said with exhaustion in his voice.

"I need… look… I don't know where to start."

"The beginning is always a good place."

"Cody, please. I wanted to apologize to you."

"And you have, so are we done?" Cody knew he should be giving Danny more time, but the resentment and anger, and the fear, were cutting deep into him.

"No, Cody, face-to–face. There's someone I want

you to meet. Look, can we meet, talk. I have a lot I need to tell you, and to ask you."

Cody hesitated. So much anger had gone before them he couldn't begin to see how they were going to get out the other side. All of his later friendship with Danny was tied to Hudson Hart, and destroyed as quickly as the connection to the band had disintegrated.

"Not now," Cody finally said. "I can't."

"Please, Cody. I'm begging you here. There are things you don't understand."

"So tell me." Cody said the words so quietly, calmly, wanting to find something that connected them again. Cody's chest tightened when Danny was silent for a long moment.

"Please," was all Danny said. "You wouldn't understand if I told you... I don't know where to start."

"You called me, you must have considered what to say if I contacted you, Danny. I might not be with you but I'm not stupid, your call has an agenda."

"Shit, Cody, you weren't ever stupid. You were the clever one... You got out before it all blew up."

"This is getting nowhere." Cody was tired of this now, all the resentment inside him settling to acid in the pit of his stomach.

"I have so much I want to say, I don't know where to start."

"You already said that once; what do you want, Danny?"

"I want to know you'll listen to me. I need you to listen to me."

Cody attempted to pull at the anger and resentment he'd held for so long, but all he felt was sadness.

"I'm listening."

All Cody could hear was Danny's steady breathing, then a heavy sigh. "I have a daughter. Cody, I have a little girl."

"What?" Cody hadn't heard right.

"Her name is Hope."

"Are you sure she's yours?" That was exactly where his head went; after two paternity cases had been thrown at him, he was instantly suspicious.

"Yes. Jesus, Cody."

Danny was a father? How had he not heard about this? Why hadn't Zee told him?

"Why don't I know about this?"

Danny sighed noisily. "No one knows about this, only Zee, and now you. Look, I'm in New York, could we meet? I want you to meet her. We could meet halfway, in Springfield?"

Five hours' drive, was Danny really that close? Last he'd known, his old friend had been in LA with the rest of the band. Safely hundreds of miles away from him.

"I'm not driving," Cody snapped.

"Still?" Danny said immediately, then he must have realized what he'd said. "Of course, I get it, sorry."

Got it? No one got it, really. Unless they'd been in the car with him, trapped and smelling gas, staring into sightless eyes, then no, they wouldn't understand a damn thing. Counseling only did so much to have him rationalizing anything in his head.

"So, you can come here..." He deliberately trailed off, leaving Danny to make a decision that was the only one he could make.

"Okay." The line went quiet again, until there was the sound of some mumbling; clearly Danny had his hand over the mouthpiece and was talking to someone else. Was it the rest of the band? Were the twins and Sam sitting there listening to what Danny was saying and wondering if Danny was the one who could get him on the television for that damn show? Was he another person out for all he could get from CJ Taylor? Was Danny going to bring the rest of the band? All of them forcing him back for these stupid fucking interviews and a freaking tour? *Stop these thoughts, Cody Brennan. Under the shit there is a Danny who used to be my best friend.*

"Danny?"

"Sorry, hang on... yes... okay." He was still talking to someone. "I can come down as soon as I'm able. I don't have an address, though."

"Zee didn't give you that?" Cody was only putting that out there as a comment, but it came off sounding bitchy. He pulled himself back in.

"No, she didn't, she said you wanted privacy... and I get that... I wouldn't ask to see you —"

"Danny, I'll see you soon. I'll text you the town name, call me when you get here."

"Thank you, Cody. I love you, man, I always will, I hope I can make you see that. Hope and I."

In the center of Cody's heart another layer of ice began to crack. Fear and disappointment shifted a little and he sighed.

Some contrary part of Cody wanted to give an arbitrary day in the future when Danny should visit, but then he realized he was losing himself in the messy maze of the crap he carried around in his head. Danny had a daughter called Hope, and for some reason he felt like he wanted Cody to be in his life.

"Cody?"

"What."

"Thank you."

"I'll see you, doesn't mean I'll go back to what we were," Cody said. And there it was, the ugly part of him pushing to the front of his thoughts. The part that wanted to lash out and hurt. "I'm not ready to go back. Not willing to put myself out there and lose someone else."

To the friendship, to the band, to what he'd left behind. Because it had nearly killed him, and he had the scars to prove it.

"I understand." Danny's voice was choked and he sounded like he was going to cry. "Believe me, I get it."

"Wait, Danny, one last thing. I won't see Katya," he said.

Danny let out a harsh laugh, but it wasn't aimed at Cody, more self-derisive than mocking. "Jesus, Cody, you didn't know what happened? Hell, you need to look me up. That's been over so long; and you were right. She was using me."

The call ended abruptly, and for the longest time Cody stared at his cell phone, wondering if he had done the right thing. He hadn't checked the Internet for details of the band or his old life in a long time. Not on a single one of his three phones, or his laptop, or his iPad. He had a new e-mail address, a new life, and there was nothing of the old one that he was remotely interested in revisiting. He'd told Zee never to tell him anything, and true to her promise she hadn't. In fact, all this nonsense about an interview and Danny was the first he'd heard in months. The last connection to Danny had been before Hudson Hart split, and that was the last time Cody had any idea of what was going on in his old friend's life.

He contemplated looking straight away, but he'd be bound to see all the old upsetting shit he'd tried to forget. The accident details, the tours, the blog commenters who'd decided he was fair game. He needed some extra time between talking to Danny and checking out the web.

He left the house, locked the door, and walked up the road to the hill. Ice on snow had him stumbling a couple of times, but finally he was at the top looking down at the lights of the town and the glints of moonlight on the black ribbon of water that wound its way through this small valley.

Closing his eyes, he formed a mental picture of Danny, of the Danny he remembered, and considered the appearance of Hope into the image he had. Would she look like Danny? Would she have his bright green eyes that stared at the world with laughter and anticipation?

When he finally walked back down to the house, he realized he had come to the conclusion he wouldn't be looking up the band tonight.

He wasn't ready for that just yet.

And he wasn't sure if he'd ever be ready.

CHAPTER FIFTEEN

Garrett tapped sharply on the table in Rachel and Megan's small lounge, and added a loud cough to underscore he wanted everyone's attention. In fact, Megan had been the only one paying attention and it took a well-aimed kick to Justin's shin to get him to listen to what Garrett was saying.

"Okay," Garrett began, shuffling papers into a neat pile. "So the venue is done, on to catering?"

"Arranged," Kyle said with a smirk. He never actually took Garrett seriously when he was in organizing mode, but no one worried. Everyone knew that at the end, Kyle would come through with whatever they needed in the way of food. "Menu B," he added at the end. Garrett nodded and made a note on the top piece of paper.

"Flowers and the slideshow?"

Megan answered for both herself and Rachel. "Done. We managed to get some more photos from Dad's school, ones that he doesn't know about."

"Collection of parents from the airport?"

Everyone looked at Justin expectantly, but he

was on his phone, or rather he was staring down at his phone, frowning.

"Justin," Megan hissed, and this time elbowed him in the side.

He glanced at her and the frown was still there, but he did finally nod to Garrett. "I'm on it," he said. He was in charge of picking their parents up from the airport and taking them straight to the hotel in Coleville, where there would be a big party for their thirtieth wedding anniversary.

"Jesus, Justin, pay attention," Garrett snapped. He'd been tense all evening, not his usual laughing self, but he had moments like this and everyone knew to back the hell off. Not so Justin, it seemed.

Justin raised an eyebrow and fought back against the criticism. "Will you actually turn up for the celebration this time, Garrett?"

Garrett pressed his lips tight, enough that Megan knew he was holding a lot back. He'd missed one party five years back and Justin had never let him forget it. Normally Justin teased his younger brother, but this time there was an edge to his words.

"I'll be there," Garrett said evenly.

"Seems to me a salesman should have more control over his vacation time," Justin muttered. He shoved his cell back in his pants.

"What crawled up your ass and died?" Kyle asked. He was sitting between Justin and Garrett, which was a vulnerable position to be in if the two brothers decided to go for the same heated debate they always had whenever Garrett was home, about where Garrett went and why he didn't keep in touch. Still, Kyle was always the one to go to Garrett's defense, and this was a scenario that had played out before.

"Nothing," Justin snapped.

"Then why are you looking at your phone?" Kyle asked.

"Leave it, K," Garrett said. He sounded tired, and when Megan looked she could see her brother seemed like he wanted to slump in a chair and sleep for a year. He'd competently steered all five of them through the planning of the big party, but now that it was done he wasn't even rising to Justin's poking.

What was it with her brothers? One of them looked exhausted and done in, the other one was staring at a phone and looking pissy.

"So we're done," Rachel interjected, her way of calling the end of this cousin meeting. She and Megan were the ones who excelled in calming everyone down, the peacemakers between brothers and cousins, but Megan wasn't sure it was working. She saw something very different in Justin, who'd looked serious and focused on the phone up until now, and Garrett, who didn't even want to join in with the annual brotherly squabble over his lack of time at home. Curious. Had they argued? Or were they angsting quite separately over different things?

She tried not to think about it; she had her own worries. The landline into the shop was dead and they needed to call a technician, and yet another slick step this morning had caused Rachel to stumble into the doorway. The weather was playing with them; not only did it mean the town was fairly dead so business was slow, but now it had caused Rachel to walk with a limp all day. Rachel swore up and down she'd salted the step again, but maybe she'd forgotten.

All Megan could think of was the cryptic comment from David about the step. He'd mentioned her falling on the step, but that would have happened early. Was David watching them in the shop? She glanced out of the window but nothing seemed amiss, no lurking exes with murderous intent. But, there was the whole moving to New York thing, and that was just odd.

Stupid. It's just the weather. It's coincidence.

"I said, we're done, right?" Rachel repeated when no one said anything.

At that second hint everyone finally made a move.

"*Call of Duty*?" Kyle asked.

"I'm in," Garrett said. "No cheating this time."

"You say I cheat; I say you're just crap with strategy."

They left, bickering good-naturedly, but not before Justin grabbed Garrett's arm and stopped him from leaving. "Sorry," he offered.

Garrett patted his brother's hand. "No problem. You okay?"

Megan couldn't fail to see the glance that Justin aimed her way.

"It's all good," Justin answered. The two of them hugged it out, and Garrett and Kyle walked off for coffee and to Kyle's apartment over Carter's Café, where Garrett often slept when he came home.

"I'm going for a bath," Rachel said. "My knee hurts like a bitch." She disappeared into her room.

Which left Megan clearing mugs, and Justin, who clearly had something to say.

"Spit it out," Megan said when Justin didn't move from his position by the door. "Is something wrong? Is it Garrett? You have to ease off on him; you know he loves his job, he can't help that some of the sales trips take him away for extended periods of time."

Justin frowned again. "I know."

"Well that is what you usually argue about, so what else has he done so that you're all up in his face?"

"Nothing." Justin fished his phone out. "It's not Garrett, it's you."

"Me?" Megan let the water out of the sink and wiped her hands on the dish towel. "What did I do?" She couldn't recall anything happening recently; in fact, the last time she'd had an argument with Justin had been over David, and that had been months ago.

Then it hit her. This was the talk, the one he always laid on her.

"That guy, Cody Brennan," he began. She shook her head. She'd been right. It was *the talk.*

She felt happy at the mention of Cody's name and decided that this was the emotion she was going with, and not to feel resentful of her brother's protective meddling. They'd had two more dates since the incident in his house, two more meet ups that involved cold brisk walks followed by dinner at his house and then hot make-out sessions on his couch, oh, and the wall by the sofa, and against the front door. She felt the heat rise in her at the memory of the way he held her against the wall, pinned her and supported her, and pushed her over the edge with his fingers inside her and kisses that melted her. They'd talked a lot about nothing much, and more than anything Megan liked sitting and cuddling on the huge sofa. They hadn't made plans for tonight; he'd said he was expecting a delivery and probably working. But that was okay, she'd had the planning meeting. Still, that didn't mean she wasn't missing the kissing and the hugging and the other bits that were getting hotter every time.

"What about him?" She sat on the sofa and pulled her legs up under her. "I'm warning you now, I like him a lot."

Justin looked pained. "You're seeing him."

"From the way you word that it sounds like you have an issue with him." She was used to that. Oscar, when she was fourteen, had been too tall and too old, the next one, Rick, too opinionated. Adam, her boyfriend as a senior in high school, was too *everything*, and then David, well, he was a conniving lying bastard. The only man Justin did like was Jordan Davis from college, and look how that had ended up— with him and Megan being friends who exchanged Christmas cards.

She waited for the summary of her latest love interest. Was Cody too much of this, or too little of that? Was he too broad, too quiet, too much of a threat to Justin's baby sister? Of course, they hadn't gotten off to a good start with Cody collapsing in Notes & Roses, but that was explained.

"This is getting old," she muttered crossly.

Justin sat next to her on the sofa. "I did a background check."

Megan went straight from relaxed to angry. That was pretty far beyond acceptable. "What the hell, Justin?"

Justin held up a hand to stop her. "In my defense, you have to remember it's a standard check when a guy collapses covered in blood and no one knows who the hell he is."

"You found out who he was, you knew he'd bought the house when you talked to Myrtle."

Justin looked wounded. "By then, I'd already started the process, Megs."

"Don't Megs me. I don't want to know whatever you think is so bad that you have to talk to me all serious, like the world is collapsing around us all."

"Megs—"

"No, Justin, okay?" She stood in a flurry of motion and grabbed her coat, pushing her feet into her sneakers. "I'm going to go up and see him and ask him what you would have found," she said. Justin was talking but she ignored him.

"Megs, come on—"

"No, seriously. Unless you can stop me here and tell me he's a danger to me, then I'll find out for myself."

Justin shook his head. "Okay," he said. "Call me, okay? I'll be home when you get back."

CHAPTER SIXTEEN

Megan had one thought in her head. Whatever Justin thought he'd discovered wasn't enough for him to stop her going to find Cody. That ruled out anything that Justin classified as too awful.

She slammed the door shut behind her and walked down the stairs carefully, then hurried past the shop, glancing in at the Valentine's display that she and Rachel had spent three hours creating this afternoon. Half flowers, with red-themed cards and notebooks, ribbons, and glitter, with the soft window lighting showing the design to its best in the dark. She walked on, up the hill and toward Cody's house, only stopping to talk briefly to Mr. Sooner and pet Bear.

When she reached the house she stopped at the front door, lifting her hand as the security light came on, then dropping it. How the hell was she going to start this conversation? "Hello, but my controlling nosy ass of a brother says he has information on you that I need to know, so for the first time I want to hear it from my current partner's lips and not from my brother. And yes, it's probably just a speeding ticket, but tell me so that it doesn't become a thing."

Or should she say *surprise*, even though he'd said they would meet up tomorrow instead because of the planning meeting, even though he'd said he was working.

He was in there playing a CD loudly, a hauntingly beautiful piano version of a recent Oscar-winning score, and for a moment she waited and listened. The music centered her and the frustration at her brother slipped away and became nothing more than an embarrassing reason she was at Cody's front door.

She lifted her hand to knock and dropped it again, turning her back to the door. This was stupid. As she stepped sideways, the security light came on again

The door opened behind her. "Megan?" he asked, standing to one side and gesturing her in out of the cold. As soon as she was in he helped her off her jacket, then captured her in his arms and leaned back on the wall, taking her weight and kissing her thoroughly with the best hello she'd had since the last time they'd kissed. They parted and he was grinning at her.

"I'm so pleased you're here; look, I have something to show you," he said, and the smile wasn't only in his eyes, but in the lightness of his step as he tugged her away from the entrance hall. He led her into the front room, and she stopped just inside the door. Where there used to be a vast empty space, except for the sofa, which the Evanses had evidently left, there was now a new dynamic. A beautiful, polished piano stood to one side, with the couch awkwardly pushed against the opposite wall. The piano was the primary focus of the room now. She looked from Cody to the piano. She recalled he'd said he played the piano, as a throwaway point that backed up his lyric writing.

"Was that you playing?" Because if it was then he was good. Or as good as she could tell with her limited knowledge of piano music.

"Yep. Come here." He grasped her hand again and encouraged her to sit next to him. He didn't touch the keys, but he laid his other hand reverently on the wood to one side. "She's beautiful, isn't she?"

"Gorgeous." That seemed the right thing to say. Warmth flooded Cody's expression.

Reverently, he traced the word Steinway in the wood. "She was delivered today."

"Can you play me something?" She shuffled away from him a little and waited. He looked at her with determined focus and then stared down at the keys.

"What do you want to hear?"

"I don't know."

He flexed his fingers and pressed a few keys, rolling his neck and playing something beautiful. She recognized the song, but didn't know who wrote it. The whole thing was classical and big and his fingers moved so fast, so confidently, but his whole body was relaxed. When he finished he gently lifted his hands from the keys and laid them in his lap.

"And?" he asked, almost shyly.

"Wow" was all she could say. She'd never sat this

close to someone playing the piano, and the vibration of the notes still played through her body. "You really know how to play."

"Thank you." He put an arm around her and hugged her. "I haven't had access to a piano for myself for a long time, but it felt right to have one here in Stanford Creek."

Megan leaned into his hold, cursing that his words struck a chord with her. Seemed to her what he was saying was that he'd never settled anywhere long enough to get a piano, but what did that mean? Should she think he was staying because of her, or the town, or should she think he was the kind of person who would up and leave without warning, despite the piano? God damn Justin and his warnings, making her think the worst.

"My brother," she murmured.

"Sorry?" he asked.

She slumped even more into his firm hold, enjoying the feel of his arms wrapped around her. He was warm and smelled wonderful, and she wanted to be here more than anything. She had admitted to herself that the idea of not seeing him tonight had been a weird one. A little missing him, and a whole lot of wanting to be with him. She hadn't been sure how to word this at the door and she didn't know how to conjure the right sentence now. Then it spilled out of her in a weird jumble of nonsense.

"So I had this boyfriend, he was called Jamie, and he was lovely. I was only fourteen so it was puppy love, but he was sixteen, and he had a car. My brother wasn't impressed, Justin that is, Garrett wasn't bothered. I think he was in his own world a lot because he'd come out and there was trouble at school. He was always being sent home for getting into fights and none of us knew how to help him. But that isn't what I wanted to say. Something about Jamie, my boyfriend, wound Justin up and so Justin, for some reason, went digging and found out that Jamie had another girl on the side, a more worldly eighteen-year-old. I was crushed, but you know, I was angry that Justin had been the one to tell me because I was a fiercely competitive kid. I had to be with two older brothers. But Justin was always the one investigating things, hence ending up as the sheriff." She stopped and considered how badly she was introducing this. Cody was smiling at her in that cautious way people did when she started talking flowers, which, let's face it, she could talk about for hours.

"Okay." Cody didn't sound like he understood where she was going with this. One-handed, he dropped the lid on the keys, and half turned to her while still making sure to have a good hold on her. It was like he sensed she needed to be grounded, had to be held.

She sighed. "Then of course, that wasn't the last time. There was this boy who Justin thought was gay, another who drove too fast, and then there was David, the doctor. I told Justin not to investigate David, but you know what, for the first time it may have been a good thing. Because it turned out David was married and all the crap he spouted about separation and divorce was blatantly not true. He was a liar and anything between us was so untrue."

"Oh." Cody didn't sound doubtful anymore, he'd stiffened a little and there was a bit of space between them.

"So, tonight Justin said he had some results on a background check he'd started on you when you were in the hospital…" She deliberately left off finishing the sentence. "But I wouldn't let him tell me, because"— she gripped his hand tightly—"I think we have something, and if you have a wife, or a fiancée, or you drive too fast, or hell, you're an undercover hit man, I need to know from you."

He sighed and tensed his hand, which she let go. His expression was bleak and he couldn't quite meet her gaze.

"I need wine," he said. "Or beer, or vodka maybe."

He stood and offered her a hand, which she took after a slight hesitation. The fact he didn't immediately deny any of the things she'd said meant that maybe one of them was true.

Good job she hadn't handed over all of her heart, although the tiny bit she'd lost to him was a part she would never get back. Uneasiness gripped her and her chest was tight. They went into the kitchen and he pulled a bottle of Chardonnay out of the fridge. One-handed, he carried glasses to the breakfast bar and took a seat. She sat opposite him, the world falling away from her. He was going to tell her he was married, or hell, something worse.

"What is it?" she asked when he didn't immediately start. "Are you married?"

"No."

"You have a fiancée?"

"No. Look, I promise you I had a valid reason for not being entirely honest. I've gotten used to keeping myself locked away tight, and up until a year back, there would have been a real danger in me telling you anything, in involving you in my life."

"Danger? What are you? A cop or something?" What if he wasn't the cop, but the bad guy? Would it change the way she felt about him? He didn't seem like a guy who would have a secret so bad it would destroy this nebulous thing they had between them. And hell, wouldn't Justin be up here arresting him or something?

He took a moment to drink some wine, a fortifying gulp that dropped the level in his glass considerably.

"I like you a lot," he said, which didn't exactly answer her question. "More than that, I want you in my life, my bed, because…"

"Because?"

"I feel like I'm already holding you in my heart."

He let the words hang a bit and she stared at him. The bed bit was a good part, but the heart analogy? Those were the words of a poet. "Oh," she finally managed. If he'd been expecting more reaction from her he didn't say, and his expression didn't change much.

"I have to tell you how I ended up in this town, but I don't want to."

"It can't be that bad."

"I don't want to say any of it, because the minute everything is out there it gives power over what we could have. That's why I didn't tell you most of it."

She didn't want to ask what the rest was, if most of it was something he couldn't say.

"My real name is Cody James Taylor."

"Not Cody Brennan."

"No, CJ Taylor." He paused like she should recognize the name. She didn't; all she could focus on was the sadness in Cody's eyes. "I was in a band once. I walked out on them; they were called Hudson Hart."

Realization hit her as she put two and two together. Hudson Hart, teen idol pop band with baby and love in every title. "I know them."

He waited a little longer and she ran through everything she knew about Hudson Hart and tried to remember what she had on CJ. She recalled twins, Zach and someone else, she knew one of the twins was gay because Garrett had this whole spiel about how pretty the guy was. There was another man at the front, she couldn't remember his name. Then Danny, she thought his name was. Why didn't she remember CJ being in the band?

"Oh," she finally said.

Cody being in a band didn't seem a thing that would scare her away. She was dating one of the guys every girl under the age of twenty-five would have once wanted to date. She sensed there was way more to this story but wasn't entirely sure how to press on.

"Is that okay?"

She leaned over and pressed a kiss to his worried face. "I can handle that," she said with a smile. None of that was making her think she should be running for the hills.

"You don't know what you're agreeing to. The Hudson Hart fan base was incredible, but some parts of it were intense. When we started, it seemed like it was only a month in and we had fans who were getting Hudson Hart tattoos. Insane. But that was okay, we were still local, we hadn't made it big."

"You had groupies and so on..." Megan tried not to sound like she was judging. She'd had exes, and expected he would have as well. Just. Maybe he'd had more than she'd expected.

Cody huffed a laugh. "I did my time, drank too much on tour, had a blast. I was still a sheltered kid from a small town when Hudson Hart released their first single; what normal nineteen-year-old wouldn't take everything he was offered? Didn't mean that after a few years it didn't get very tiring. We were clean-cut, no drugs, adoring girls, we played on the moms liking us too. Made quite a bit of money as well, but I left before they hit the arena shows and got bigger."

"Why did you leave?" she asked curiously.

"Tired, and I had a paternity case thrown at me, and to top it all I was being sued for a song in which I'd allegedly reused lyrics written by someone else." He worried at his lip with his finger, and then sighed. "It was all bogus. I wasn't the dad in the paternity case, and I had written the lyrics and the case was thrown out. But you know what…"

"What?"

"I didn't even remember sleeping with the woman who shouted I was her baby's daddy, and for a while I doubted it was me who had written the lyrics. I was losing control of myself, so I pulled clear. I just did it too late for it to matter."

There were a lot of questions she had about both, but instead she focused on the fear in Cody's eyes. There was something else, a darker secret he wasn't sharing with her. And that unnerved her.

"What happened, Cody?" she asked.

He grimaced and pushed away the wine, stepping back until his back was against the opposite counter. "I had a stalker," he began, then held up his hand. "No, I don't want to start there."

"Okay." Megan stayed encouraging.

"We all had those fans that went too far; it's part and parcel of what they made us, of what we all thought we wanted to be. All that potential money, and exposure, and the fact it was up to us to strip off our shirts at the drop of a hat. We were no One Direction, but we were a group of kids who were happy to play the game. I wrote lyrics; that's what I am good at." He raised his hopeful expression to Megan. "I'd written everything for Hudson Hart, but I never wanted to be in the band. I fell into it because my best friend, Danny, was invited to join."

"How old were you when you joined?"

"I was nineteen, same as Danny, the others were

eighteen. We did some shopping mall shows, local stuff, got picked up for a one-record deal. I don't know why, maybe 'cause I was the quiet one, or the one who didn't push himself into the limelight, but I got these stalkers, weird guys and girls who wanted to know more about me. Followed me, wrote me, tried to kiss me, that kind of thing."

Megan made a small noise of encouragement when Cody stopped.

He cleared his throat, emotion catching at his voice. "Then someone accused me of stealing the lyrics like I said, and it was a court thing. I was exonerated, but not before it had lessened what I did, and made me feel like maybe I wasn't as talented as I thought I was. A big blow for any cocky kid who thinks they're gifted. The case took a year, the stalking crap was doing my head in, the album wasn't coming together because I couldn't write, and I was fucking it all up. I had one stalker—Julia, her name was—and she was blatant about what she wanted, and even though the cops were involved and there was a restraining order, it escalated. Add in the paternity case and hell, I was finished."

"So you left? The band."

"Not then. I'd worked so hard at helping them, and wanted to be the best I could be for my friends. Then Sam, he met a girl, and he fell for her like nothing I'd ever seen before. He was twenty and he'd fallen in love."

Megan imagined she saw the way this was going. "And she was a stalker as well?"

"No. God no, Leah was lovely, older than Sam, but soft and sweet and he fell so hard. Julia, the stalker, was all mine, one of our engineers. She was a psycho. Julia Ortiz," he spat the words, and hung his head, clearly unable to continue talking.

Megan went with her heart. Nothing he'd done could be as bad as what he imagined right now in his head. She rounded the breakfast bar and slotted herself between his legs, cradling his gorgeous face and hating the sadness in his eyes.

"Go on," she encouraged.

"I was planning on driving Leah home, a favor to Sam, because he was running late for a fitting for the big tour. You know, the one where we did shopping malls, and stores, and small shows. I'd done my fitting, and what would it hurt? Leah was a good friend to us all, and I was going that way anyway." He stopped and closed his eyes. "We were driving away and Julia rammed us. She was on us in seconds, and there was no way we could get out of the way. Security was there, but they came over too late. I was holding my hand over Leah's wounds, a deep gash in her chest, trapped in the car, and Julia stood, with blood on her, and she was pleased that Leah was lying there, dying, shouted she was a whore for fucking me and that she was Sam's girl, not mine."

"Oh God, did Leah die?"

"Someone called 911, and we got her to the hospital. But it was too late."

Megan's heart twisted in her chest. That was horrific. Poor Sam, poor Leah. "Oh my God," she whispered, and pressed a kiss on each of his closed eyes. "Did they have to cut you out of the car?"

"Yes. It took an hour, maybe more."

He was playing down the fear, she could tell that from his words. He'd been trapped in the car, a woman bleeding out beside him, another taunting them. It must have been horrific.

"They kept out of the press that I was even there at first, and that was the wrong thing to do, because within three days it came out, and the secret of it all was so much worse than what had actually happened. Because you can't keep secrets, not now, not when every move people make is on social media. Was I driving too fast? Was I not looking? Even Sam questioned me, when it was nothing to do with me."

"I'm so sorry."

"Everything died down, Julia was eventually put away for murder, but it was the final straw. I tried, I really tried, but my head…"

"Okay…"

"I left the band because everything was just"—he opened his eyes and they were bright with tears he was holding back—"everything was wrong. Panic and fear itched and scratched at me and I was right to leave. I couldn't look Sam in the face, and how stupid was that, he wasn't blaming me, but I was having a pity party for one."

"What happened next?"

"The company medics attested I was unfit, I was scared and miserable, depressed, anxious. The counselor said I had PTSD."

To her mind it sounded like he was ashamed of all of that, and she didn't know how to explain to him that he shouldn't feel that way. She couldn't say that to him, though. As it was he seemed edgy and she didn't want him to run.

"But the tour went ahead."

"I left the band, they took my lyrics, Tyler's music, and they hit the big time, enough so that their first album sold well. I'm a footnote to Hudson Hart. The locals in San Diego knew me, I even had fans across the country, but it was the twins, along with Danny and Sam, who had the limelight. A footnote is where I belong and I like it that way."

Megan saw how he reduced what had happened to him to nothing more than a few paragraphs. How was it possible to work through so much fear and grief and remain sane?

He pulled up his sleeve and tilted his arm so she could see the tattoos clearly. A twist of dark bands that climbed his arm. "You can see the scars if you look closely."

She peered at his arm, at the maze of interconnecting lines that she wouldn't have spotted had she not been this close. She ran her finger over them. "What did this?"

"My arm went through the side window; the glass cut into the skin." He took her hand and pressed her fingers to one line that wasn't smooth. It bisected from inner elbow to the back of his arm. "This was the worst one. I lost blood."

She pressed a kiss to the mark and realized she

was holding back tears. The pain he must have felt and the horror of what he'd seen...

"I don't remember the accident in the news," she said.

"They focused on Sam, on the fact he'd lost his girlfriend. Zee was good at that. There was no point in using my tragedy if I wasn't even going to be in the band. Right?"

"That's cynical," Megan said.

"True, though. There's a big market in grief out there and I didn't want to be part of it. Sam didn't either; he was devastated, lost, but he stayed the course and somehow he was stronger than me." Megan didn't want to point out that she thought Cody was the strongest man she'd met. Instead she changed the subject.

"You changed your name."

"Changed it back, you mean. I was never CJ, not really. CJ was a product of me and Danny attempting to be cool."

"Danny was in the band. Danny Hudson. And Sam is Sam Hudson, Danny's brother."

"Yes, my best friend, and my best friend's brother."

She wrapped her arms around him and rested her cheek against his chest, hearing his heartbeat against her. She wanted to ask whether they talked, whether they were still friends, whether Cody felt like now he had reached peace of sorts.

Instead she just held him.

CHAPTER SEVENTEEN

Cody was relieved. Megan hadn't run screaming out the door, despite the fact she must have a million questions, which he promised himself he would answer. Everything was so raw inside him. Sam hadn't been able to look him in the eyes for a long time, the grief in them both too much to handle. Sam never blamed Cody for Leah dying, but there was a significant point in their lives where things had changed between them.

And as for Danny, they hadn't talked for ages, and Cody doubted they had anything to discuss even now. Apart from his daughter, Hope, of course.

He held Megan close. How could he tell her, after all that he'd told her, that he was falling for her? He'd come off as needy and pathetic.

"I'm not obscenely wealthy," he blurted out, hiding his face in her long hair where she couldn't see him. "Not the same as the rest have, but more than I need if I'm staying at home just writing, from writing royalties I mean."

She chuckled against him. "Damn, there goes my need for a private jet."

"I have royalties, though, on songs I wrote, so that's a good income," he added.

She tugged away and tipped her chin to look at him. Her amber eyes were narrowed. "Why are you telling me this?"

"So you know I'm not a complete waste—"

"What the hell? I fell for the guy with the beard and the blood," she said with a quirk of a smile. "I assumed he had a shopping cart with beer cans in it."

"You couldn't have fallen for anyone in that situation."

She wrinkled her nose. "I saw your eyes, all blue and pretty, and so full of pain."

"My eyes, right," he said with an answering smile.

"So," she said, and stepped back and away out of his reach. "Why are you still hiding?"

She had a point. He hadn't quite explained why he was never staying in one place for any length of time. There was still that little shadow in his life he doubted he'd ever be able to shake.

"Letters. I get them from fans, and every so often they scare me enough to make me want to run."

Did admitting that make him look like less of a man to her? Should he lie now and say he liked moving places all the time?

"And have you got them here?"

"No. Everything is forwarded to my agent, Zee. Last she had was the morning I walked into your shop covered in blood and stinking of vodka. She called me, I reacted badly."

"But you stayed."

"No one knows I'm here yet, the letter was forwarded from my old rental place."

"But you bought a place in town; seems like you wanted permanence of some kind."

"Less of a trail if I'm not renting," he said with a shrug.

"I get that." She nodded like she understood, but some of the light left her eyes.

He'd said something wrong and he knew it. He should have said that since he'd met her he didn't want to leave, that he wanted to stay here.

"And you," he blurted out. What was it with him not being able to control his words today? *Idiot.*

She looked puzzled.

"You," he said again. "I want to stay here and see you, kiss you, every day. I like you, and I want to see if I can try being normal for once."

She considered his statement with care. From the expressions on her face, she went from confused, through pleased, and on to shy. Then she pulled her cell from her jeans and fired off a text.

"There, that will stop Justin and Rachel worrying."

"What did you send them?"

"See you in the morning," she said in a soft tone. Then she placed the cell on the counter and took his hand. "We should talk more about this. In the bedroom."

He tugged her to a stop. "Really?"

She went on tiptoes and pressed a kiss to his lips. "Less talking, Cody."

They stepped into Cody's bedroom and he crossed to the small bedside table and flicked on a lamp. The room filled with soft light and she had her first look at the enormous bed that took up most of the room, flanked by the cabinets, with one large closet in the corner. There was a door which she knew from her time here as a kid led to a half bathroom; other than that the only other thing she noted was the thick dark drapes at the window.

He came back to her, resting his hands on her shoulders gently. "I can't believe this," he murmured.

"What?"

"That I have you here." He slipped his grip down her arms and around to her hips, sliding up and removing her loose top. She helped him, raising her arms and wriggling free. Not exactly sexy, but there was time for sexy. He chuckled as he helped untangle her hair, and they laughed when she couldn't quite unbuckle his belt.

This was them, and it was natural and flawless.

Finally with her in only her bra and panties, and him only in boxer briefs, they stood close to each other and the heat of Cody's skin was like a furnace. She traced his chest with her fingers; he had little chest hair and two cinnamon nipples that she scraped across with a nail, loving the small hiss he let out and the way they pebbled under her touch.

"You like that?" she whispered.

He didn't answer at first, reaching behind her and unhooking her bra, cupping her freed breasts and kissing each nipple reverently. The touch was fire to the core of her.

"You like that?" he asked as she arched into his touch, willing him to close his lips around her.

"Mmm," was about the limit of words at that point. She feared that if she started to talk, all she would do was beg.

He edged her backward, her calves hitting the bed, and carefully, *gently*, he lowered her back and helped her scoot up a little until they were both lying on the top covers. He straddled her, grasped both her hands with one of his, and the action lifted her breasts. He spent the longest time sucking on them, tasting them, his other hand always busy, stroking soft lines down her skin. Every so often his fingers would dip below the lace of her panties and her breath stuttered in need. But he never pushed lower, just around, gently, pressing, until she was pushing up against his hand hoping it would slip down, wanting him to touch her. He moved up a little and this time the kisses trailed from breast to lips. And all the time he wouldn't let her move freely, and his fingers moved closer to the center of her.

She wanted him to be the best lover she'd ever had, she wanted him to be slow, but firm, to know exactly how to touch her, she wanted him, no, needed him to be perfect. The kisses deepened and he slid his fingers under the lace, brushing the hair there, a little bit of pressure, enough to have her near whining into the kiss. He moved to the side of her, still grasping her hands, pinning them flat, and somehow he rested on one side, moving and using his knee to encourage her legs apart. She didn't need to be told twice; her legs spread, her left knee bending, and she tilted a little toward where she could feel his hand. Just a centimeter more, nothing but a breath from touching her, and she wanted it so badly.

"Beautiful," he murmured between kisses. "I want it all."

He tugged on the lace, the material sliding against her, a small amount of pressure right where she had to have his hands.

"Cody, please."

"What, gorgeous girl? What do you want?"

"Your hand, please…"

She arched again. The pull of the lace, and the press of his finger, and she could feel the ripples of her orgasm close, each one sliding and building. He pushed the lace to one side, sliding down a little, sucking on her nipple and testing the inside of her with a finger, his thumb massaging the soft outer skin. She closed her eyes; this was too much, he was too much, she was liquid fire and so close.

"Show me," he said, soft and low. "Show me what you want."

She pressed down on his fingers, arched her breast into his mouth, and all the time he praised her, pushed her, and demanded she feel everything. Finally it was too much, every sensation centered on him, and with a cry she crashed over the edge and sobbed her relief.

He held her, not moving. The sensation would

have been too much; he just kept the pressure and he kissed away her quick breaths, finally sliding his fingers from her, and slipping the lace away.

He rolled on a condom, all the time looking at her, watching her, and she reached for him, running her hands down his length and caressing him beneath the latex.

"I need you inside," she murmured.

He settled between her legs, moved up, pressing against her, pushing inside, slowly, coming back onto his knees and bringing her with him, holding her steady in his arms. He was almost too deep, and she adjusted her position, the rub of him enough to have sensations curling inside her. She'd never had this before; this mindless need to come again. It had never happened this way before. He rocked into her, kissing her, wringing pleasure from every stroke.

"Touch yourself," he whispered as he broke the kiss. "Show me where you want to be touched."

She knew without a doubt that if she touched herself it would be game over; she was on the edge again and she wanted to go over. She waited, seeing his eyes close, feeling the change in the way he thrust into her, and she reached between them, three fingers pressing against them, feeling where he was inside her.

He shouted as he was coming, and then kissed her deep and hard, and she pushed against herself, and tipped her head back with a cry.

"Cody," she whimpered, her oversensitive skin on fire.

Gently he laid her back on the covers, removing and tying the condom and dropping it in the trash. She was still wet, and for a second he looked at her, pushing apart her knees and pressing a kiss to each hip bone.

"I've never seen anything so beautiful in my life," he said, before kissing his way up her body and to her lips.

They kissed lazily for a few minutes, until post-orgasm tiredness stole over her, and wrapped in his arms, she slept.

CHAPTER EIGHTEEN

When she woke it was to complete darkness, but she knew instinctively that it was time for her to get up. Ever since buying into Notes & Roses she had an internal alarm clock that woke her at six.

"You okay?" Cody whispered to her, pressing a kiss to the back of her neck. She shuffled back against him.

"Need to get to work," she said, sleepy and so wishing she could stay in bed.

"Can't you phone in sick?" Cody teased.

"Nah, the boss is a bitch." She turned in his arms and snuggled against his chest. "But I have an hour for a shower and coffee."

"Hmmm, we could share the shower, if you like. Conserving water and all that."

They stumbled bleary-eyed into the bathroom. By Megan's calculation they had managed about three hours sleep last night, and she was going to need a lot of coffee to get through today. Particularly as it was Valentine's in two days. Lots of last-minute orders, and some work she could do in advance on the bouquets. Lost in thought, she used the new toothbrush she'd been handed and Cody disappeared off to give her a bit of privacy before coming back with two huge fluffy towels.

He turned on the water and, gloriously, sexily nude, he waited for her to go in first. The cubicle wasn't huge, and shower sex wasn't her thing—too much water and not enough room—but kissing? She could do that forever.

Which was why it was a surprise when she ended up with her legs wrapped around Cody's waist, in the throes of her first orgasm of the day, his fingers inside her and her nails digging into his neck, the blessed warmth of the water against her back. He moved a little, pressed her against the tiles, and kissed away the hiss she made at the cold contact. Pushing her there, he lost himself to his own completion, groaning into the kiss, the evidence of what they'd done washing down the drain. They stood this way for a while, just holding each other.

"We need to buy condoms and store them in here," she announced as soon as her breathing steadied.

All Cody did was kiss her deeply and chuckle. "We can do that."

They dressed, and kissed, and had breakfast, and kissed, and drank more coffee, and oh God, the kissing was so good. Then when it was time for her to walk down to work, she saw he was pulling on his coat as well.

"I'll walk down with you, get you coffee from Carter's," he said in explanation when he caught her staring.

"If you get Rachel hot chocolate she'll love you forever."

"With extra marshmallows."

"You're a smooth mover, Cody Brennan."

Together they walked down the hill. There hadn't been any fresh snow overnight but the banks of cleared snow either side of the sidewalk were high.

"In the summer this place is beautiful," she said.

"What I see now is beautiful," Cody replied. She glanced at him and realized he was staring at her. She punched him lightly in the arm.

"We get a lot of tourists."

"So, in the summer this place is packed with people?" He sounded disappointed, like he hadn't known Stanford Creek's main income was the summer visitors. Evidently he hadn't done his research on the house he'd bought.

"Without them Stanford Creek wouldn't survive," she explained. "What we make during the summer months from the tourists keeps us going through the winter."

By unspoken agreement, they stopped walking at a small lookout halfway down the hill. From there the river was visible still, even though some of it was behind the shops and houses of the town. Beyond the river, the bridge over into New Hampshire was empty of cars, and white on either side from snow. Cody released his hold on her hand and turned his back to the view, with the fence supporting his weight.

"I can't be here in the summer," he said. His blue eyes were focused on her, and she saw questions and regrets in their depth that he couldn't put a voice to.

The spell of the two of them making love, and being together, with all the possibilities for lots of tomorrows, was broken. Megan's heart sank. She'd not felt disappointment as acute as she was feeling at this moment. The way he spoke it seemed like he was putting an end time to his stay here. What did he mean? Was it just that maybe he had work in the summer somewhere else? Or a place he had to visit? To her ears it sounded terminal.

"Why?" she asked. He looked down at her, a frown marring his handsome face.

"With all the people. I don't do people," he said.

"They're only here during the day," she began carefully.

"One of them could see me, and then that gets put on Twitter, or Facebook, and then what? I'm not safe anymore, and neither is anyone with me. I like the isolation here at the moment."

"This might be a small town but that doesn't mean someone wouldn't recognize you and post photos of you."

"I get that, I'm not ready to make a stand quite yet."

So why say you're falling for me? Why make it sound like you might be interested in staying here? What am I, just a month of dating and then you're gone?

Megan didn't say any of that. "You bought a place here," she said instead.

Cody answered with another of his enigmatic

shrugs that said absolutely nothing. "We'll cross that bridge when we come to it. Right?"

He offered a hand and she took it. She wanted to say that she would go where he wanted for the summer months, however impractical that was, but were they ready for that final leap where she said the words written on her heart? *I could love you, if you let me.*

They rounded the corner onto Main, past Carter's, the sign in the window showing it was shut. The fact her generally early cousin hadn't opened the place up at what was now seven thirty didn't immediately worry her. No, what worried her was the group of people outside Notes & Roses. Justin was there, in uniform, his back to her and Rachel by his side, and there was Kyle, and it was he who noticed her. Slowly the family parted and she stepped into the space, Cody still holding her hand.

What she saw shocked her. Glass destroyed, the Valentine's display iced over, the shop open to the elements, and in Justin's hands a large lump of brick.

"What happened?"

Justin turned the brick to show the note that was attached with garden twine. She read the word out loud. "Whore."

"What do you know about this?" Justin asked.

"I don't know anything," Megan said, realizing she wasn't processing it well. The single word in black pen, smudged from frost, didn't seem real at all.

"I wasn't talking to you, I meant your boyfriend here."

Cody tightened his grip on her, pulled her to his side. "I don't know anything."

"Wait," Megan said. "The alarm, why didn't it sound?"

"Cut," Garrett said as he joined them from the entrance to the parking area and Megan's apartment beyond. He held up wire cutters. "Alarm line, phone line, destroyed." He looked utterly focused, not wavering in his stare at Cody and Justin.

Cody pulled out his cell and dialed a number, holding it to his ear. "Zee," he said without introduction. "I need to know where Julia Ortiz is… okay… you checked… who did that? Thank you." He ended the call, and looked directly at Justin. "We need to talk."

Justin huffed loudly. "Damn right we do. Spill."

"Here?"

"You see me moving?" Justin snapped.

Cody deflated a little. "Julia Ortiz isn't behind this. She was my stalker, and she's still in prison. Although why I even thought she'd be out…"

"Why did you have a stalker?" Rachel asked. She was bundled in a huge dark parka and looked as shocked as Megan felt. She wanted to get inside the shop and assess what they'd lost. Call someone to fix the window. Anything except stand there and feel scared, talking about how Cody's past could be something to do with this.

Justin pointed at Cody. "Rachel, meet CJ Taylor. He used to be in a band called Hudson Hart."

"Way before they made it to the big events," Cody interjected.

Rachel blinked a couple of times, looking at Cody, and Megan felt sorry for him. Was this what it was like to be under the microscope, like a bug pinned to a card?

"Wow," Rachel finally said. "I don't see it at all. You used to be all..." She waved her hands, but Megan wasn't sure what her cousin meant. "You used to wear much less in the way of clothes," she finally finished.

Justin interrupted. "So why is someone throwing bricks through my sister's window?"

Cody shook his head. "I promise you, if I thought it was anything to do with me..."

"It isn't," Megan said. She wanted to stop everything before it escalated out of hand. "Garrett, can you call someone about getting wood to board up the window? Rachel, let's get inside and tidy up some, see what we can salvage. Kyle, open your damn café, we all need coffee." She released her hand from Cody's and glanced up at him. He wouldn't meet her gaze so she cradled his face with her gloved hands. "And you? Get the coffees from Kyle, and help me. Okay, Cody?"

He blinked at her and then focused in on what she was saying. "Coffee. Okay."

Cody stepped back and away, following Kyle. Garrett stepped away and was talking on the phone about wood. Which left Rachel and Megan looking at the wreck of the shop window and the display.

Justin didn't move either; he looked from the shop to Megan and back again.

"I don't like this," he said.

"We're not exactly dancing with excitement," Rachel snapped.

"Who would do this?" Justin asked. "David," he added.

Megan sighed. "I don't want to think that. I just imagined he was an idiot, not a psycho."

"What if he did it to stop you delivering, or to scare you into doing what he wanted?" Justin was pushing for her to admit what she had already begun to suspect. The flowers delivered, the guy sizing up the shop to sell, slashed tires, even the slick icy steps that had been cleared before. Was it possible David was not only an idiot, but someone who would go this far?

Justin sighed heavily. "Liam called me this morning. He said he'd been ordering in replacement tires. Why didn't you tell me someone slashed your tires?"

"I drove over something," Megan protested. "It was an accident." Even as she said it she saw the investigator in Justin putting two and two together and making five.

"Liam said not, he said it looked like someone had deliberately slashed the tires."

"What the hell?" Rachel asked.

Justin placed his hands on Megan's upper arms and held her firmly. "Look at me," he instructed. Megan looked up at him, seeing the fear in his eyes. "Megan, I need you and Rachel to be aware, okay? I don't know if this is something to do with Cody, or that somehow we have someone else in the equation."

"I promise."

He released her and turned to Rachel. "Promise me, Rachel."

"Okay, okay." Rachel held up her hands in defense, and both she and Megan watched him walk down toward the coffee shop, following everyone else.

Megan surveyed the damage. "So, we need to clear this up, and either you or I have someone wanting to send a message."

Rachel put her hands on her hips. "Well, shit," she said with feeling. "Best get started, then."

Megan couldn't agree more. They opened the front door, neither of them removing coats, and regarded the mess from the inside. No snow overnight meant the area inside wasn't saturated with snowmelt, but it was iced and cold and as the ice became water it would cause a lot of damage. There was nothing that could be kept from the window display, save some ribbon that had fallen to one side and remained in perfect curls. Didn't matter, it was the first thing Megan pushed into the recycling boxes. As they worked to clear the mess there was a comfortable silence between them—until Rachel asked the one thing Megan had been waiting for.

"So you're dating someone in a boy band. When were you going to tell me?" She sounded a little hurt, but then how was she to know that Megan had only just found out?

"Ex-boy band, and he told me last night, after

Justin threatened to tell me himself after running one of his freaking background checks."

"Wow," was all Rachel said. They carried on cleaning. The stock in the stationery side was mostly okay, cold, but only the items closest to the window were damaged by the damp cold from last night. A van pulled up, and two men got out with wood and nails and anything else that needed doing.

"We can get a glazier here for this afternoon," they said. But not to Megan and Rachel, instead to a glowering Garrett, who covered the mouthpiece of his phone, said something to them, and watched them work.

"I bet he scares people into buying whatever he sells," Rachel said. They exchanged tired smiles and returned to the clearing up.

After what seemed like an hour but was probably only twenty minutes, Cody arrived back with the coffees and the chocolate for Rachel. The wood was up at the windows, a temporary solution and one that darkened the interior.

"Hudson Hart then." Rachel began the inevitable conversation. "The CJ that left and broke up the band."

Megan waited for Cody to snap at Rachel, or grimace, or dip his head, anything except the grin he gave her. He'd apparently decided that the persona he was showing Rachel was the lighthearted *nothing is too awful* one.

"Yep, all my fault, they couldn't survive without my baby blues." He fluttered his eyelashes and, like that, the tension broke. Until Rachel asked the very thing that had been on the tip of Megan's tongue.

"When do we get to meet the rest of the band?"

Cody shrugged and bent over to pick up the largest of the recycling boxes, easily hefting it up into his arms. "Someday," he said. Then he jumped the two steps to the street and disappeared. Rationally Megan knew he was only taking the trash to the collection area behind all the shops, but the softer side of her saw a man who wanted to avoid talk of what he'd used to be.

"That man is damn complicated," Rachel said, with a moue of disappointment.

Megan wanted to say something flippant, like "tell me about it," or "damn right," but all that came out was exactly what she'd been holding back from Rachel since she'd seen her outside the shop. Some things you couldn't keep from your best friend.

"I'm falling in love with him."

Rachel straightened and rested both hands on the display she'd been emptying.

"Really?" she asked.

"Uh-huh."

Then Rachel smiled, a broad grin that danced in her green eyes. "Well, shit."

CHAPTER NINETEEN

Cody pushed the last of the destroyed flowers into the compost bin and forced them down to replace the lid. He didn't know what to do now. To go back to the shop meant confronting what had happened, seeing the evidence of what had happened. What if it was something to do with him?

And it probably was. Megan had lived in this town her entire life, and he bet she'd never had a fucking brick through her window, or had her tires slashed

His neck itched, and he got the sense he was being watched, but a cursory glance showed nothing. He was paranoid and that paranoia he'd pushed so far down had done nothing but rear its ugly head over the last few days.

I thought falling in love would be the easy part.

"You probably need to leave."

The words made Cody turn, tense and ready to fight, relaxing when he saw Garrett glaring at him.

He had a million things to say in his defense. That despite the fact anyone could reveal he was in this town, he wanted to make a stand here. He'd lied to Megan so she didn't get her hopes up, but it wasn't worth the hurt in her eyes to consign her to a few months here in Stanford Creek. He wanted to stay because he was falling in love, because he wanted to keep Megan safe, in the same way she was making him feel safe. He wanted to fight this one, but all that came out instead was a simple, "I know."

"You've been seeing my sister for a while now. Maybe a month, give or take a day. Probably best you stop that now and run away again. What do you think?"

Cody was about to agree when the tone of the question and the way it was worded hit him in the gut. Was Garrett asking him to make a stand here? Suggesting that running was a bad thing to do?

"Cat got your tongue?" Garrett said.

Justin sauntered around the corner. "You found him," he said. For some reason Cody felt like this was going to end badly, with him up against the dumpsters and two broad guys looking to go all alpha on him.

"I love Megan," Cody said, keeping his comment simple. "And if this is my fault or not, I'm not going anywhere."

Justin folded his arms over his chest, and Garrett chose a similar pose. If Cody wasn't feeling quite so worried about what had happened, he might have laughed. And then Megan was there, shoving Justin, making him stumble, and punching Garrett in the arm, before slipping past them to stand next to Cody.

"What the hell is going on?" she asked. "None of this is Cody's fault, and he's not going anywhere." She looked up at him and waited pointedly.

With a wry smile he pulled her close. "Nope, not going anywhere."

Justin opened his mouth to talk but shut it again, and side eyed Garrett, as if to say, *all yours.*

"Okay then, let's work out what the fuck is going on here."

"Zee told me, that's my agent, she said there'd been another letter. They think it was from the woman who was convicted of the murder of Leah, her name is Julia Ortiz. The letter is signed and everything, but Zee did say the signature didn't seem the same, and it wasn't to this address."

"Stalkers in prison wouldn't be allowed to get letters out to the people they stalked."

"I know."

"She's in prison," Garrett observed. "You're right to feel safer."

Justin frowned at the words, but he didn't disagree. How could Cody explain what having a stalker was like? Moments where he felt safe were few and far between, and somehow the threats and actions scared him and made him feel less of a man.

Cody hugged Megan closer. "She also said there is a sister who made some noise about appealing Julia's case, but that it never got off the ground. Could it be the sister who is causing the trouble now? Could she have targeted Megan? I didn't even know she had a sister," Cody said, shaking his head.

"You didn't know about a sister?" Justin sounded incredulous, and why wouldn't he. Cody had reached a point where he shut everything from the case away from him. He'd stopped paying attention. Stopped listening. Just stopped everything.

He looked from one brother to the other. "You have to understand, I left it all behind. The house, Zee, the band, everything, I don't even check the web for anything to do with my old life. All I remember is that there was no sister in court, and I thought it was over when Julia was locked away. You have to understand... I had a breakdown."

He stopped. Admitting that to the two most important people in Megan's life was hard. Add in the fact Megan was next to him, and this was stripping him raw. He'd been pushed to the edge by the court case over the lyrics, defending his artistic integrity, thinking he was losing the respect of his peers, wondering if he was worth a thing. Then add in the stalking, not only from Julia but people sending personal notes that made him jump at shadows. He'd lost control of his life. Hell, record company medics had attested to his state of mind, pulled him off the statewide tour with Hudson Hart. *So how did he put this into words?*

"I was... this is me, here in Stanford Creek, running away." He was brutally honest now. Justin nodded once, and Garrett relaxed a little. As if his admission was what they needed to here.

"It's okay," Megan reassured. "We'll sort this."

"I'll follow it up," Justin announced, and left.

"I'm going with him," Garrett said. At the last moment he turned at the corner, and looked back to them. "So, question for you, Cody."

"Yep."

"Is Tyler single?"

Cody huffed a laugh. "Tyler Hart? From the band? You know, I have no idea."

Garrett smirked and left the two of them standing in the most unromantic place in the whole of Stanford Creek: the trash area.

"You okay?" Megan asked.

"Shouldn't I be asking you that?"

"I'm worried about you."

Cody kissed her, a soft gentle promise of a caress. "Let's get this shop fixed up."

Holding hands, they rounded the corner, and the flash of something caught Cody's eye, a light, metal, he wasn't sure, but the growl of an engine was enough to have him alert. In a second he saw what was happening. An old Toyota was heading straight for the shop, a glimpse of someone in the driver seat, and a flashback to another time. He and Megan would be crushed, and he yanked her, using his entire body strength to push her away, pivoting on his foot and shoving hard.

The impact of the car was the last thing he felt, the cracking and crashing and a scream.

Is that me screaming?

And then, blessed silence.

CHAPTER TWENTY

Megan hit the ground hard, her shoulder smacking into the sidewalk, and her hands grabbing at air. She screamed Cody's name as he shoved her away. There was a screech of metal against stone, and she couldn't see him.

"Cody!" she shouted as she curled up and moved to her side, pushing herself to her knees. Hands grabbed at her, yanking her back, and she fought like a wildcat.

"Megan, stop it!" A voice in her ear ordered. Justin was shouting at her, trying to pull her away from the car embedded in Notes & Roses.

"Rachel! Cody!" Megan struggled again, but more hands held her, this time Garrett as well. The wheels of the car that faced them were still spinning, the front right corner up in the air, and the nose of the car solidly into the wood of the window.

"Dispatch, I need paramedics, and fire, on the scene, now."

Justin shouted the words, and they buzzed around her head. She struggled again. Rachel was in the shop, the front of it destroyed, and under that car, somewhere, was Cody. Steam rose from the shattered front end of the car, and a figure slumped over the steering wheel, the airbag half inflated.

She yanked herself away, getting two steps before Justin lifted her bodily in the air.

"Stop it, Megs," he ordered. Then Kyle was there, taking over, pulling her back and away, his arms around her.

"Let them work," he said.

She struggled as Garrett and Justin clambered over the car, assessing the damage, and saw Garrett slide off the hood and into the shop. Seconds later he called out that he had Rachel and she was okay. Megan didn't believe it until she saw Rachel climbing over the hood, helped by Garrett. Which left Cody.

"Let me go!" she shouted, wriggling again, an expert at escaping the holds of her brothers and cousin. Slipping free she stumbled forward, and as Justin reached into the car to assess the driver, she slid to her knees. Cody had been standing right in front of the window, and he could be pinned. She crawled forward, as close to the spinning wheel as she could, Kyle right behind her.

"Don't go in there, Megs." Kyle tried to stop her, but she had to see.

The engine died. Whether it was finished or Justin had managed to cut it off, she didn't know, but the wheel stopped spinning and she reached past it, desperate to get under the car.

"It's not safe," Garrett shouted as the car shifted

a little and piles of debris rained down on her head. She sensed Kyle move closer.

"I've got her," he said, bracing the car with his back, even though she knew that was futile if the thing moved.

"Go back," she said.

"Megs, no."

"Go back." Her hands met a leg, and she knew this was Cody. "He's here, go back and tell the fire guys." She had to think rationally, assess what was there. His leg. She wriggled under. Someone touched her foot.

"Get her out of there." Justin's voice.

"We can lift the car together," Garrett shouted.

"We can't; if he's pinned, we have to wait. Megan? What can you see?"

Instinctively she drew her foot up so she wasn't being held, and moved even further in. Cody was curled in on himself.

He didn't seem trapped at first, but then she saw he was pinned with one leg between the car and the wall.

"He's pinned under the car," she shouted back to her brothers.

"Fuck," Garrett snapped.

She crawled that bit further, and she could reach his face.

"Cody, talk to me." He didn't move. He couldn't be dead, not when she'd just found him. She shimmied closer, ignoring her brothers shouting for her to come the hell back out.

She touched him, pressed fingers against his pulse point, looked right into wide-open blue eyes, and saw the tremulous smile.

"Hey," she said.

"Are you okay?" he managed to force out.

"I'm all right; they'll be here in a minute to help you."

He attempted to move and let out a low moan. "I can't feel my leg," he said. He looked scared, and she leaned closer, resting a hand on his chest.

"It's numb from the pressure."

"Should never have come here."

Megan's heart twisted at the words. "Cody, stop trying to talk." He looked white, his hands in fists gripping at his jacket.

"My fault, the driver was trying to get to me…"

"No one's fault, Cody, this was an accident." He attempted to move, gasped, and closed his eyes. "No, no, keep your eyes open, Cody, look at me."

He did as she said, opening his eyes and blinking at her. "So beautiful," he said. But his words slurred together. This wasn't good. She couldn't see blood on his head, but that didn't mean anything.

"Fire crew is here, get out of there," Justin shouted, a hand at her ankle again. "Get out, Megan, we need to get to Cody."

"I have to go," she said. "I love you, Cody Brennan, don't you shut your eyes."

He stared right at her. "Keep my eyes open," he murmured.

"All the way open. Promise me."

"I promise…"

She pressed a kiss to the bare skin at the base of his throat, and then even though she didn't want to, she crawled back the way she'd come, catching her clothes on metal and stone until it bloodied her, and finally out and into Rachel's waiting arms.

"Is he okay? Is he dead?" Rachel asked, tears tracking down her face.

"He's alive," Megan said. Rachel helped her to one side, the fire crew stabilizing the car. As the car lifted she realized they were cutting the driver out. She couldn't see who it was. Was it an accident, or had someone deliberately targeted them? She wrenched free of Rachel's hug and rounded the car, ignoring the firefighter who attempted to stop her, coming up on the paramedics trying to resuscitate the driver. Abruptly everything made sense.

David.

David was driving the car, aiming directly for her, for Cody.

She stumbled toward him, and he looked right at her, a gash deep into his face, blood everywhere.

"Knew you'd be there," he said and closed his eyes, arching up in pain.

She saw the paramedic working on his airways shake her head. With the amount of blood and trauma to his face, it was a wonder they even thought he could be helped. Looked like the air bag had done little when the car had hit the bricks.

"Oh my God, David," Rachel said in disbelief by her side.

"He knew I would be there," she repeated. "He meant to hurt me."

Megan stumbled backward, onto the road, and sank to her knees on the blacktop, her breath catching, every fear she'd ever felt sapping her energy. Justin hadn't moved, right in among the first responders, and Garrett was only a few feet away. Kyle came to stand with Rachel and together they watched as David's body was covered, and the car was lifted an increment at a time, the paramedics calling to stop and then start.

As soon as it was physically possible, the smaller of the two paramedics scooted under the wrecked Toyota and from this position she could see the other crouched down and gesturing for the fire crew to stop lifting.

Cody was pinned, what if that was the only thing keeping him alive? What if moving the car led him to bleed out? What if that gentle kiss she'd placed on his throat had been a goodbye?

"No," she groaned. Kyle knelt on one side of her, Rachel the other, and they watched as the responders worked.

"Everything will be okay," Kyle reassured.

"You don't know that," Megan said on a sob. Someone put a silver blanket around her, and she gripped hard to the shiny material as finally they had Cody on the gurney. Megan immediately attempted to stand, her limbs frozen in place, relying on the strength of everyone else to get her to Cody's side. The paramedics had done something complicated with his left leg, bound it, elevated it, and there was urgency in getting him inside the ambulance.

"I'll be there," she shouted at Cody. But he didn't open his eyes, and he didn't say a word.

She began to run toward the hospital, the ambulance overtaking her, and her breath was harsh gasps, her progress slow, her left arm a mess of cuts and blood, and the pain in her wrist a sharp edge of agony. Garrett reached her, helped her to stumble the last bit of distance. They'd already taken Cody out of the ambulance, and somewhere in there was the man she loved, fighting to stay alive.

They were known here, nephew and niece to the doctor in chief, and they were shown to the nurses' lounge immediately, friends from school who now worked there crowding them. Justin came in the door, looking shocked, harried, and with urgency in every step. Megan stood to ask him what had happened and he gathered her into a hug.

"It's going to be okay," he said.

She wished she believed him.

When the news reached the place that it had been Dr. Collins who had crashed a car into the shop and had died on the scene, the ripple of shock reached nurses, orderlies, and staff alike. When accident became deliberate attempt to cause damage and hurt Megan, the grief became anger.

And all of it was nothing; all of it swirled around Megan and chipped away at her, until she was going mad with wanting to know what was happening to Cody inside the room.

Her aunt pushed into the nurses' break room. "They said you were here," she began. Then, without hesitation, she explained: "He's okay, fractures, some internal bleeding, nasty wound to his thigh, but a couple of days and he'll be out of here."

Megan had stood as soon as her aunt entered the room, and abruptly the strength left her. She slumped into the chair and winced as she knocked her arm, sickness climbing inside her.

"Get her to X-ray, Garrett," Aunt Lindsay said.

"Not going anywhere," Megan said, a stubborn need to sit right there until she could see Cody backing off the pain.

Lindsay crouched in front of Megan. "Baby, you need to get your wrist seen to."

"I want to see him," Megan said on another sob. "Make sure he's okay."

Lindsay sighed. "I've never lied to you before and I'm not starting now. He's going to be fine. Get your wrist seen to and as soon as it's done I'll take you in myself."

She followed a technician to X-ray and allowed her arm to be manipulated to get the best images. As shock was wearing off, the pain was getting worse. Added to that the technician wasn't talking to her, wasn't even looking her in the eyes. Was everyone going to blame her for David dying? How could that make sense? She couldn't worry about that now; the man she'd dated, albeit briefly, was dead, and the man she loved was in a hospital bed.

She stood up when the technician said she was

done and assumed she'd be told where to go next. She'd never broken a bone in her life, and even though she was an expert in finding her way to long-term care and maternity because of her job, the parts of the hospital around casualty were all new to her. Instead, the technician stopped her at the door.

"I wanted to give you..." She hesitated, looked everywhere other than Megan.

Megan was too tired and in too much pain to listen to anything right now in the defense of David.

"Whatever it is, I had nothing to do with what happened. He killed himself."

The technician, Felicity according to her badge, looked up, "God, no, of course you had nothing to do with it. I just wanted to tell you that I was sorry this happened, but that no one here liked Dr. Collins. He had a way about him that wasn't quite right. Would send these expensive gifts and guilt a woman into being with him." She shuddered. "Creepy."

Megan sighed. "Thank you," she said. Whether she wanted to hear that or not, it was probably going to help.

"I know one of the other pharmacy technicians, Angela, she was very close to filing an official complaint in. He wouldn't leave her alone, talked about taking her with him to a job in New York. And she thought there were drugs involved. I don't mean to speak out of turn, but I wanted you to know."

The two women exchanged nods, Megan holding back the irritation of the pain in her arm.

Felicity snapped back to professional. "Right,

let's get you to a nurse and get this arm seen to."

They found a nurse, and Felicity stayed while she was being seen to.

At first, the nurse was quiet, and then she seemed to find the words she wanted to say.

"I never liked Dr. Collins," she blurted out. Then she blushed, and wouldn't look Megan in the eye. "Sorry, but he was a creep who couldn't keep his hands off the nurses."

"All talk," Felicity added.

"Did you hear what he did to…"

Megan tuned out the conversation. The rational side of her knew she was in shock, but she was docile and allowed herself to be tended to. All the while she wanted to find Cody, to see him, to touch him and make sure he was okay. The break was bad enough that the wrist needed setting, and when she finally found Aunt Lindsay, Megan was buzzing with pain meds.

"Sit somewhere," Lindsay said gently. "I'll come find you and take you in to see Cody."

She wandered over to the waiting area where Garrett was taking up two chairs. He stood the minute she walked in, and opened his arms wide to her. She walked into the hold.

"Sis, I'm so sorry," Garrett murmured into her hair.

"I'm okay. Cody's going to be okay."

"I don't know what David was thinking, why he would do that."

"He said he knew I was there. This was deliberate."

"You think he put a brick through the window to make sure that at some point you'd be standing in front of the store? Christ. I thought he was a fucked-up idiot, I didn't think he'd be capable of hurting anyone."

"No one could have known."

"Did he ever hurt you before this?" Garrett looked down at her. "You can tell me if he ever made you feel... uncomfortable."

"David? No, I would have told you, or someone. But there's a technician here and he was using all the same lines on her." Her voice was muffled by the fact she'd buried her face in Garrett's jacket again, but evidently he could hear and understand her.

"Okay, we'll tell Justin."

"Why did he do it? Why would he try to hurt me?"

"We might never know."

"Do you think it was because Cody kissed me in front of him? Is it our fault?"

"No." Justin's voice had her turning in Garrett's arms. "More to do with the meds we found in his locker, a lot of black market hallucinogenic drugs, and copies of letters from New York hospitals telling him his applications were unsuccessful."

"Was there a note or anything?" The idea of suicide and taking her with him wasn't something she wanted to even think about, but it was one possibility.

"Nothing." As though he knew that would be hard to swallow, he added, "I'm sorry."

"I just thought he might have wanted us to know something."

Justin changed the subject. "Have you been in to see Cody?"

"I was told to wait here. Aunt Lindsay will find us."

Justin sat down opposite them. "I have a call in with his parents and sister."

Megan nodded. "They would want to know if... if he..." She couldn't finish the sentence and hunched over in her chair. They sat that way for the longest time, and she only looked up when a voice interrupted the introspection.

"Excuse me? Could you tell me where I'd find the patient waiting room?"

A tall man carrying a car seat stood uncertainly at the door. He was wrapped in a huge coat, beanie, and scarf and had apparently come in from the cold without stopping to strip off.

"Back out and turn left, then left again," Garrett answered him.

Tall man looked relieved. "I got turned around and ended up in Maternity; I think they thought I was donating a baby." He looked nervous and flushed, and as if to underscore that he had a baby in the car seat, the little thing let out a piercing wail. "Sorry."

He was apologizing a lot and for a second he stared at the car seat, then the seating, then looked down at himself.

"You can stay here," Garrett said. "This isn't the official waiting room but it's quieter for the baby."

"Thank you." With a visible full-body sigh the man took off the beanie, unwound the scarf, and shrugged off the jacket. His dark hair was short, but his bangs long enough to tuck the bulk of it behind his ears. Then dipping his gaze he sat down and scooped out the baby from the seat, along with a bottle from an insulated bag. Deftly, he settled the mewling baby, and Megan watched the whole thing. She couldn't help it. The man was someone she recognized.

"Are you here for Cody?" she asked.

He looked up and directly at Megan. "Yes, I'm…" The baby snuffled and he looked down.

"Danny," Garrett finished. "Danny Hudson."

Danny nodded and looked at the door marked Staff Only. "What happened? I called him to tell him we were here—"

"You spoke to me," Justin interrupted.

"Sheriff Campbell?"

"Yes."

"You told me you had Cody's phone. That I should come here."

"Hit and run, or rather, someone drove a car directly at my sister and Cody," Justin said simply.

Danny looked pale and then just as abruptly he had a fierce expression. "Is that someone under arrest?"

"Dead," Garrett said flatly.

Megan closed her eyes briefly. None of this was real.

"Good," Danny said, just as calmly and concisely. "Is Cody okay? He's not going to… I mean… I don't know if I deserve to be told…"

"You'll know when we do," Megan said.

Danny relaxed a little. "Thank you."

"Cody told me about what happened in LA," Megan said.

"All of it?" Danny paled.

Megan didn't know if she'd been told everything, but enough to know one thing she could tell Danny. "I know he still thinks of you as a friend."

"He does?"

"Despite everything."

Danny sighed heavily. "Fuck," he cursed with feeling. Then winced and cast a look at the small baby in his arms. "Don't listen to Daddy," he murmured. Then he turned his attention back to Megan. "Are you okay? I mean, I can see your wrist is in a cast."

Megan held up her wrist. "Cody pushed me out of the way," she said. She could do this. She could be composed and focused and not lose it altogether. "He grabbed me when he saw the car, and he planted his feet and shoved me away. He didn't..." Her voice wobbled a bit and she swallowed against the tightness in her throat.

"It's okay," Garrett said, grasping her other hand.

Megan looked at her brother and the compassion in his eyes pushed her over the edge. "He didn't stand a chance. He was pinned between the shop and the car."

Silence. Absolute silence.

"They would have told me... wouldn't they... if he was..." Danny's voice cracked. "He's not dead. He can't be dead." The words weren't a question and tears filled Danny's eyes. Megan was quick to explain.

"No, he's in there and he's alive."

Danny sagged with relief, but he straightened himself when the baby in his arms gave a muffled squawk. "Hear that, Hope," he murmured to her. "You're going to meet Uncle Cody."

Megan didn't want to be sociable anymore, and slumped forward in her seat, her head bowed. All she wanted, was to see Cody.

Now.

CHAPTER TWENTY-ONE

The pain had receded, and in its place was a warm fuzzy floating feeling that Cody enjoyed for a little while before reality hit him.

Pain and horror, and Megan, and the car hurtling toward them. He knew Megan was okay, she'd talked to him, said she loved him. But where was she? Panic made him moan and fight against whatever was lying on his chest making it hard to breathe. He forced his eyes open, blinking at the light, and attempted to focus on what was around him. He was getting damn tired of hospitals. There was nothing on his chest, but the tightness and pain were nearly at his limit.

"Megan!"

A voice was close by. "It's okay, Cody, she's okay, your girl has gone out for some pain meds."

Cody looked to the left, his neck muscles protesting the movement. Was there any part of him that didn't hurt? The last person he was expecting to see was half up out of the visitor chair.

Danny.

"She's really okay?" he managed to get out from his dry cotton mouth.

Danny grabbed a cup and supported Cody's head as he encouraged him to sip some water. Grateful for the blessed cool liquid Cody closed his eyes as he drank.

Danny eased him down and placed the cup back on the table.

"Her wrist is in a cast, that's all. She's nice. I like her." There was a pause. "Heard you got all heroic and pushed her out the way of the car."

"What are you doing here?" Cody asked. His voice sounded steadier, and the humming in his head was subsiding.

"Visiting, remember? Only I get here and all I see is a car in a shop and stories about attempted murder and that you're mixed up in it all."

He heard voices, and one in particular. "Megan."

Danny smiled wryly. "We'll talk later." Then he did something totally unexpected. He pressed a hand to Cody's chest, right over his heart, the pressure firm and unyielding. Cody winced; it fucking hurt. "Be well, Cody. I missed you."

Then, before Cody could even think of a reply, Danny left and in his place Megan leaned over him and kissed him, the warm touch of her lips on his enough for him to reach for her and draw her closer.

"Don't mess with your ribs," she teased. She twisted and sat next to him and he attempted to scoot over to give her more room, only making himself gasp in pain as he did. He didn't even know what he'd done, what had happened, any of it. All he remembered was that Megan was okay, he'd managed to push her away and she'd talked to him, said she loved him. Only the thought of that, of the words she'd spoken out loud, was enough to terrify him at the same time as making him feel like the luckiest man alive.

"I love you, too," he whispered. "But…"

She placed a hand on him, just like Danny had done. "There's no buts where love is concerned," she said back just as quietly.

"Someone tried to kill me, and instead they got you."

"Cody—"

He grasped her hard and winced at the pain. "No, I won't do this again. I won't let anyone hurt you."

Megan kissed him, hard enough to stop him talking.

"He was aiming for both of us, Cody."

"He?"

"David."

"The doctor." Cody sighed and gripped her hand tighter.

"He's dead. Killed on impact."

"I'm sorry he died." That was going to be so hard on Megan, to know that the man, albeit deranged, had died by smashing into Notes & Roses.

Megan was quiet and she didn't answer; instead she gripped his hand so tight that he winced. "He could have killed you."

Cody lifted his other hand to touch her but the cannula attached to something in a bag was enough to stop that motion.

NOTES & ROSES   247

"He could have killed you too."

Tears welled in her eyes, but she didn't cry. Instead she curled into his side and they lay there together. Safe.

Justin came in to report, but Megan was sleeping, her unhurt hand still tight on his. He looked serious and focused.

"What's wrong?" Cody asked.

"More news," Justin said. "Just got out of a meeting with the trustees. David used drugs here. They've audited and found prescriptions he'd written for fake names; very slick move, no one suspected him, and wouldn't have until the next full audit at the end of the month. They're so understaffed that things slid. They're looking at Aunt Lindsay as to where the buck stops."

"Shit."

Justin shook his head. "She's already working as many hours as she can, she can't be held accountable for the failure."

"I wish I knew what to say."

Justin looked so damned defeated. "I know."

"Why did David want to hurt Megan?" Cody murmured. Megan shifted in her sleep and he smiled down at her. Who would ever want to hurt her?

"Fuck knows." Justin pushed his fingers through his hair and grimaced. "He had nowhere left to go, talked about New York but nothing was going to happen there. I don't know what he wanted, but maybe he saw Megan as his last chance, and when it was obvious she was with you…"

"My fault," Cody said without self-pity.

"Stop that," Justin snapped. "This was no one's *fault,* David was a dangerously confused man under the smooth exterior. If it's anyone's fault it's mine for not doing a better background check on him once I discovered he was married. A bit more digging and I could have maybe saved everyone from this shit."

"You couldn't have known. Not even the hospital knew what he was doing."

Justin shook his head. "I tracked down David's wife in rehab an hour back. Apparently David was a heavy user of pain meds, that's the reason they split."

Megan stirred, stretching a little. "Justin?"

"How you feeling, sis?" he said and pressed a kiss to her forehead.

"'M okay," she mumbled.

"I'm working with Aunt Lindsay, get well quick," he said. Then with a nod and a grim smile to Cody, he left.

The door closed behind Justin and Megan twisted to sit up, releasing her hold on his hand. "Sorry, the meds knocked me out."

Cody moved his arm to encourage her closer; the pain was manageable and he needed her as close as possible.

"I love you," he whispered.

"I love you, too."

"Sleep now."

His parents were there when he woke up the next time and, just behind them, his sister, with tears on her face, and his nephew in her arms.

Megan wasn't there, and he was bereft, uncertain how this was going to go down. His dad was stoic, his mom encouraging, but it was his sister's reaction that made his heart swell.

"Never again," she said. "I will not be pushed away for my safety again. You understand me?"

Cody felt a curious mix of relief that she didn't hate him, and a fear that there were horrible things in this world that could hurt the people he loved.

Ben, his nephew, stayed nervous for the grand total of five minutes before clambering onto Cody's bed and demanding to know all about ouchies. For a four-year-old he was very perceptive when Cody explained a bad man had hurt him.

"Mom says bad people want to hurt you, but she wants to help keep you safe."

Cody's heart shifted a little at that, his chest tightening. He had hugs and love and, even with the pain, he wanted his family to know how much he loved them, by never letting them go.

Zach and Tyler sent a gift basket, a curiously garish affair filled with all his favorites, from Jack Daniels to licorice. Sam sent a card, signed with his name and a single sentence, *Time to have a drink together, I think.* Maybe the two of them could sit without the specter of Leah and sadness between them.

And Danny? He sat with Cody every so often, sometimes with Hope asleep in his arms, sometimes on his own, but only when Megan wasn't in the room. Cody put off talking about serious things until he didn't feel so fogged with medication, and Danny never once mentioned the reason why he was supposed to be visiting.

"You wanted to talk?" Cody said, after three days of polite conversation in which Danny watched him carefully.

"Now?"

"No time like the present."

Danny paused. "It's about Hope."

"What about her?"

"I need to talk about Katya first." He held up a hand to stop Cody talking. "Did you look up what happened?"

"No, nothing."

"We married, divorced, she got pregnant in between, with Hope. I convinced her not to have an abortion, had to promise money, hell everything, for her not to do anything stupid. You were right, she didn't have a heart."

Cody hesitated in his response for a moment. Danny had summarized a lot of shit happening in one sentence, but he seemed okay. Focused on his daughter. Cody's chest tightened at the thought of what his friend had gone through.

"I didn't want to be right," Cody said in his defense. "I'm sorry she hurt you."

Hope was a quiet baby, content to lie on Danny's

chest and sleep. Apart from some mewling when she got hungry or needed changing, she was the perfect baby. Not that he had held her at all; his chest was still completely fucked and the faint edge of pain was his constant companion.

"It is what it is," Danny said tiredly. "I signed it all over, everything, any investments we had, the house in San Diego, and in return I have a divorce and Hope, free and clear."

"She didn't want her?" What mother didn't want her baby? He couldn't understand.

"She's moving on to the *next big thing*. Didn't even want to hold Hope when she was born."

Cody couldn't understand a mother not loving her baby, but he knew it happened in life. Not everyone was cut out to be a mother.

I wonder if Megan wants a family?

"But Hope has her daddy, and her Uncle Cody."

Danny bit his lip and nodded, his eyes bright with unshed tears. "She needs you, we need you. Your help."

"How, what can I do?"

There was a soft knock, and then Megan came in. She was carrying coffee, and Cody near whimpered at the thought of the heady brew, but the coffee wasn't for him. She handed one to Danny and sat on the visitor chair with the other one.

"Hope is sleeping; Cody's mom is spoiling her with cuddles," she announced.

Cody glanced at Danny. "You were saying?" he prompted.

Megan made to stand. "Sorry, I didn't mean to interrupt."

"Stay."

"Please stay." Both men spoke at the same time. She subsided in the chair.

"Can I have just a small amount of coffee?" Cody asked a little desperately.

"Doctor said no," Megan said.

"Torture," he said to the room, his eyes narrowing as Megan smiled at him.

"Tomorrow, as soon as you're home, I'll get Kyle to make you so much coffee you'll be floating to the ceiling."

They exchanged smiles.

"We can talk later," Danny said.

Cody had almost forgotten his old friend was in the room, and coughed to cover his embarrassment. "No, Danny, I'm listening."

Danny swallowed and sat forward in his chair. "I'm not telling you this because I want... look... hell, I don't know where to start."

"From the beginning," Cody said.

"Hope was born with a congenital heart problem, and she had a small operation when she was born and we thought everything would be okay. She was so tiny, but they didn't have a choice. Katya had left by this time, and I spent every hour I could watching Hope, praying she'd be okay." He slumped a little, the weight of his memories pushing him down.

Cody didn't know what to say. "God, I'm sorry, Danny," He finally offered.

"I think the hardest thing was seeing her so small in the NICU, with tubes and…" Again he stopped, bending his head and sighing heavily.

"I wish I'd been there for you," Cody said.

Danny nodded and looked up. "I wish you'd been there, too. I'm sorry, Cody, that I didn't listen about Katya, that all I saw was the better man telling me what I should do with my life."

"The better man?"

"The one who saw through the shit, and got out of it all."

A moment passed between them, one that needed hugs but, with Cody stuck in bed in pain, that wasn't happening soon. Instead he extended his fist and Danny gently fist-bumped him.

"She'll need more operations, more help, and Cody… I don't have anything left. Nowhere to live, no money left."

"The poor thing," Megan said. "What can we do to help?" She leaned forward in her chair, her hand on his leg, and she looked at Danny with so much compassion.

The compassion that Cody should have always held for his best friend. The connection that he'd lost because his head had become so screwed up with the stalking, the accident and the case against him about the lyrics. Maybe if he'd talked to Danny at the time…

"You need money? Time? A place to stay? Anything," Cody added. "But… I can't go back to the old life; I can't put myself out there in the public eye."

"I know, I understand." Danny nodded, his expression changing from anxiety to optimism.

"But anything else, okay," Cody said. "Count me in."

And he meant it.

EPILOGUE

"So I looked you up on the Internet, you, and the band," Megan said from the sofa. She'd curled up there earlier with her iPad and decided she'd chill the rest of the day. She'd been at the shop in the morning and the repairs were well underway but, after six weeks, she'd not been long out of the cast and last night her sleep had amounted to about two hours—she had to get used to not rolling over and hurting her wrist.

Of course, the lack of sleep was also Cody's fault. Yesterday he'd been cleared by the doctors, and last night he'd shown her exactly how much better he was, and she'd enthusiastically joined in.

"You did?"

"Have you seen some of these promo shots from when you started?"

She tilted the iPad screen to show him one of the shots from when he looked about twenty. He was sitting on the piano stool, his fingers resting on the keys.

"Just a kid," he said.

"You haven't played the piano yet, even though

you could." She decided being direct was the right thing to do.

He shrugged and Megan sighed to herself. She'd been trying to get him out of the melancholy in which he seemed sunk today but nothing was working.

"Oh. My. God. Look at this."

He glanced over and smiled at her when he looked at the next photo. She'd deliberately chosen a shot of all five of Hudson Hart, and all of them were bare from the waist up. Cody, broody and serious, had jeans on, hanging low on his hips, and she got a very good look at the hipbones and indentations that she loved to kiss.

"We were all so young," he said. Then, turning back to the piano, he stared down at the keys.

"Says here you love Chinese food and your favorite color is blue."

"Used to be," Cody muttered. He sighed audibly, "Zee said Julia's sister has admitted sending letters on her sister's behalf."

"Will she be arrested?"

"I don't know. I'm not sure what is going on anymore."

Megan laid her iPad on the cushion and moved to sit next to Cody. She hip checked him to move up and peered at the music. He'd shown her where a *C* was on the keys and the sheet music. Given she didn't have a musical bone in her body she felt pretty damn pleased with herself when she managed a chord that sounded okay.

The noise was loud in the otherwise quiet room.

"That's a *C*," she said confidently.

Cody shook his head. "That's not quite a *C*."

She peered down at the keys, gauging the layout and pressing a chord again. "There you go, a *C*."

"No," he took her hands and guided her, but she didn't quite do it right. "I'll show you." He placed his fingers correctly and connected to the ivory. A *C* turned to another note, and she scooted away a little to give him room, listening to the notes building together to form a melody she recognized.

He wouldn't know she deliberately fluffed the note just to get his fingers on the ivory.

He finished the piece and half turned to her. "I needed that," he said.

"Of course you did. All those notes are only the start."

Cody closed his eyes briefly. "You know the day in the shop, when I collapsed?"

"Not going to forget it in a hurry."

"I was looking for the notes," he explained. "I saw the word and in my head the music was inside the shop, but you want to know something?"

"What?"

"The notes weren't in the shop, they were in me. I needed you, somehow, to show me how to find them again."

They kissed and the kiss was a promise of more.

"I love you," Megan whispered into the kiss.

"I love you, too," Cody said with a smile.

"Can I ask you a question?" Megan asked between kisses.

"Sure."

"What is your favorite color now then? You said it *was* blue."

Cody stood, took her by the hand and pulled her into a hug.

"The color of your eyes."

"Light brown?" She'd seen her eyes in the mirror; they weren't a color at all; well, nothing she could label.

"Gorgeous, sexy, amber, come-to-bed eyes."

Megan swallowed at the heat in his words. She stood and held out her hand. "I think we need a nap."

"It's early."

"It's never too early for a nap," she said firmly.

He followed her and chuckled. "We're not sleeping are we?"

She stopped just inside the bedroom, stealing a heated kiss. The she broke the kiss and looked up at him, her arms wrapped around his neck.

"Nope. No sleeping today."

ENJOY THIS PREVIEW OF THE SECOND BOOK IN THE STANFORD CREEK SERIES, *LOVE AND HOPE*!

Rachel is cold to love, until Danny and Hope show her how to live.

Danny has found a place for himself and his baby daughter to live. Hope is everything to him, and he would do anything to keep her well and safe. From getting her well to dealing with the fact his ex-wife is back in the picture, his life is one huge mess of worry and fear.

There is no room in his life for relationships, or love, but meeting Rachel, a woman with secrets in her eyes, is enough to have him thinking things that he shouldn't.

Rachel has parts of her hidden away, things that she doesn't even want to admit to herself, let alone her close-knit family. Dating the wrong guys is one way to protect her heart, but falling for the enigmatic Danny, and his beautiful daughter, could change all that.

Can Danny and Rachel ever get past the reasons why they think love isn't possible and realize that actually, love is the only thing that matters?

CHAPTER ONE

"That's enough, Eric," Rachel said with a soft smile to let him down gently.

Rachel sidestepped her date with graceful ease, a little coyly, and a whole lot avoiding her date's wandering hands. She didn't want to upset him; he was on his seventh beer, and that was just the ones she'd seen. He was unsteady on his feet, and his surface shine had certainly vanished in the two hours they'd been at her aunt and uncle's anniversary party at the restaurant. The sit down dinner had long since ended, and the day had segued into an evening of dancing, drink, and party food.

"C'mon," Eric slurred, petting her arm and slipping to cup her breast. She swatted his hand away, and he frowned.

Not for the first time she regretted her impulse to bother with a date. She didn't need one, Kyle didn't have a date tonight, and she could have spent the whole evening with her brother and no one would have said a thing.

"Eric. This is a family party."

She pushed at him, almost playfully, like she

didn't really mean it. No point in causing a scene and having her brother and cousins descending on her, to defend and berate at the same time. She could deal with these. Eric DeLaney just needed air, and probably six black coffees. And if she could get him in the garden then he may well cool the hell down.

"I want a kiss, sexy," he said and pulled her in for some tonsil hockey right in front of her parents.

"Let's take this outside," she said with her best alluring smile, breaking the kiss and ignoring the frown on her dad's face. At least her dad disapproved quietly, unlike her brother who had spent five minutes telling her Eric DeLaney was a complete asshole.

Which, let's face it, he was. Eric was way too eager to get out of the party and paw her, but anything was better than her dealing with it in front of everyone, kicking him in the balls and taking him down.

"And then we can kiss, right?" His voice was erring on the whiny side and not for the first time tonight; Rachel considered why the hell she'd thought bringing Eric, the idiot, as her date. He was a no-hope loser from Stanford Four Corners, visiting a cousin or some such story, and she'd decided he would be an easy to pass off date. They'd been at school together, him a few years above her, captain of the football team, limited academic achievement, blah blah. Typical kind of idiot she dated, really.

But he'd asked her out, and she'd said there was a party, and he'd jumped at the idea of a free bar.

And maybe, this time, she'd end up kissing

someone that didn't make her sick to her stomach. A small part of her where hope lived was the thought that Eric wasn't a dick to the core, and that he was just misunderstood.

She was wrong.

He was the very definition of hot, tall, built, and with an impressive line in tips on which *boring* team would win which *dull* tournament. But there was nothing between his ears, other than sports stats, and there was certainly not a single spark between him and Rachel.

Which was exactly how she liked it. She only dated to look normal to friends and family. Normal was something that was critical to her, in her ordinary life, and her regular town. Normal meant no one asked too many questions, or made her search for reasons why she wouldn't try and find a guy she actually even liked.

So, she'd give Eric one kiss, and send him on his way with a pat on the back and a *see you later, big guy.* Getting serious with Eric, or any man come to think of it, was not on the cards. The sound of a baby crying filtered through the cooling night air and Eric glanced in the direction of the noise, allowing her to get past him.

"No kissing tonight, Eric." She caught her stupidly high heels on a paving stone, and it slowed her down enough so that Eric held her arm. With remarkable agility which belied his size and drunken state, he got in front of her and pasted what he probably thought was a cute expression on his face.

"Baby. One. Just one."

Rachel sighed. Eric was not going to stop. She opened her mouth to discuss rationally why she wasn't kissing him, but the words left her in a huff as Eric gripped her upper arms. He shuffled her back into the darkness against the fence and pressed her there, and she was squashed between the wall and the heavyset man.

"Eric, come on, stop it, you're drunk," Rachel said, a lot louder, and one hell of a lot firmer. He grinned down at her like this was one big game to him.

"C'mon baby, one kiss."

"Eric!" Rachel attempted to shove against him, but she couldn't get purchase in her heels and toed them off as best she could.

"No one can see us," Eric muttered. "So fucking hot, I want you out of that dress."

A dozen scenarios went through her mind, all the Krav Maga techniques she'd learned to take care of herself. The quick sharp movements that kept her life under control. The first step of which was stopping action before escalation. She'd failed that part, thought she'd had control over the laughing drunk guy who just wanted to dance. Until, that is, he wanted fresh air and a kiss. The next, the physical force, she was trapped awkwardly. That left talking and getting him to move back just enough so she could get purchase.

"C'mon, sweetie, not here," Rachel said in her best girly tone.

He didn't move, just nuzzling at her neck, sucking at her skin. No fucking way was he marking her skin, and she shuddered at the thought of his teeth on her.

Too many shadows in my head. Too many memories that won't leave me alone.

"Let's go somewhere else," she said.

"For more than kissing," Eric said, with a chuckle as he pressed his erection against her stomach and she insinuated her hands between them. All she needed was a pivot point, and she could get him off her, but it would take some time.

"My family is here," she said, still smiling up at him, even though panic began to filter into her thoughts. She desperately attempted to focus on sounds and smells around her, the baby crying, soft talking, the music filtering outside from the party, the scents of spring in the air. Anything to find peace.

"We can go in a minute, I want to fuck you here, right here," Eric said. "So beautiful."

"No."

"C'mon, sexy, you could just suck me off."

"Eric, get off me," she said with more force. He still didn't move.

"You should let her go," a voice said from their side.

Eric looked sideways, tensing as he did. Rachel felt his muscles bunch, realizing this was going to be quite a bit harder than she first thought.

"Fuck off, pretty boy," Eric drawled. "Get your own one."

"Let her go," the man said again.

"Not your fucking business," Eric said, this time with added snarl.

She didn't recognize the new voice, and couldn't see who it was, given her head was smushed up against Eric's chest and turned the wrong way. It didn't sound like her brother, though, or Justin, or Garrett, thank God. All of them would, in turn, yank Erik off, beat him into a bloody pulp, and then lecture her, and she'd stand there and take it like she always did, because she had no choice.

Choice had been taken from her, violently, brutally, and with utter finality a long time ago.

"Let me go," Rachel snapped.

"Step away," the man she couldn't see said again. He was closer, or he was talking louder. Either way, she recognized that voice and her shame was complete. Danny Hudson.

"And I said, Mr. Millionaire, that you should fuck off." Eric rested back on his heels, and just that gap was enough to allow her to twist her hands, and kick with her foot to his shin followed up by a knee to a groin as he stumbled back. With a shout of pain, Eric fell to his knees, cursing a storm.

"I. Said. No," Rachel kept her tone even. She didn't raise her voice, couldn't even face Danny directly who was standing *right there* with a sleeping baby in his arms. She could see him move closer in her peripheral vision, hand outstretched, probably to help her, or to reassure her? She didn't know, but she didn't need another man's hand on her right now.

"Fucking cock-tease," Eric cursed, pushing

himself to stand, but not going any nearer.

"You're drunk, Eric," Rachel said patiently.

"I've wasted a whole night on you," Eric said. "I bought a fucking suit," he added, a little more pathetically. He stepped toward Rachel and she tensed, sideways on, ready to take him down if she needed to, even though he'd passed from horny to affronted. He must have sensed her intention; either that or he was so drunk that he wasn't focusing on what he wanted.

"It's okay, Eric, you can go now," she said with patience, even though she felt nauseous and angry. *Calm the situation, pay attention to the cues.* The only cue Eric was giving were ones that screamed he was pissed.

Then he threw his hands in the air, stumbled at the momentum, and caught himself with another curse. Then he deliberately addressed Danny, pointing at Rachel and sneering.

"No fucking way you're getting inside the ice princess," he snapped. Then without another glance, he walked away, limping as he did.

The words hurt. Not just because Eric called her ice. But that he was exactly right, she was ice. Inside, she was frozen.

"Are you okay, Rachel?" Danny asked. "Do I need to get someone?"

Rachel couldn't avoid looking at him, and wished she hadn't. He looked was past worried, his mouth pressed into a tight line and concern written in every line of him. He used his free hand to push back his bangs which had the annoying habit of falling over his eye, jiggling the baby as he stood. Not that she'd been watching him push back his hair for the last few weeks, or that every time she saw him holding Hope her chest tightened and she couldn't breathe. Ever since he'd arrived in Stanford Creek, he'd been right there insinuating into her life. He was friends with Megan, shot pool with Kyle, drank beer with Justin, and charmed everyone he met.

Gorgeous, lithe, muscled, with his floppy dark hair and stunning blue eyes, he'd caught Rachel's attention, not in a sexual way, but in the way you'd stare at something to learn more about it. She was curious about the man with the child, and the air of sadness that followed him everywhere. Add in the fact that he seemed like a genuine guy, despite his career as a singer with a band, and he was an ordinary man.

Well, as regular as was possible for someone with his eyes, and his body, and the fact he could sing, and dance, and had an adorable kid, and held a cloak of vulnerability around him.

The damn man was everywhere. Only yesterday she'd gone to Megan's house and found Danny sat on the sofa with Hope asleep on his chest, and it was all Rachel could do to turn straight back around and leave. She knew he was staying with her cousin, but to see him in all his sexy cuteness, hugging Hope, and looking at Rachel with a welcoming smile on his face, was too much for her to handle.

She could almost imagine desiring a man like him

or, at least, the person he pretended to be. She liked to think she could see through everyone's masks, but Danny was an intriguing mess of opposites. Quiet, but funny, sad, but happy with his child in his arms, he was contradiction central.

Desire? That wasn't anything she was going to feel again. She'd not been a nun since college, by any stretch of the imagination, but she kept things light and the men she was with knew the rules. One night only, no sex, and then done. Thinking of an alternative to that was impossible. She blamed being close to Megan all day, every day; proximity was messing with her psyche. Just because Megan had a man to herself now in Cody, didn't mean Rachel wanted one.

I don't ever want one.

I can't *ever have one.*

"Rachel? Can you hear me? Are you okay?" Danny asked, and she was aware she'd gone mute, still staring at the arch Eric had limped through.

"Of course I am," she said. "I can take care of myself."

Danny finally quirked a smile at her. "So I see," he said. Hope squirmed a little, her soother dipping out of her cute rosebud mouth, and he cooed at her and pressed it enough so she could find it and latch on. "I wanted to help, to get him off you; I couldn't help because I had Hope…"

"Like I said, I don't need any help," she said.

"Okay." He was smiling at her now. "You want me to get someone? Your brother? Or Justin?"

Horror flooded her, not just at the idea of her brother getting up in her face about the choices she made, but to add the sheriff in the mix, despite the fact he was her cousin, was a step too far.

"God no," Rachel said, heat in her tone. She made a show of brushing herself down, even though there was nothing there, and still Danny didn't move. Was he waiting for something else? She searched her head for something to say, but social graces escaped here, particularly when her heart was still racing from Eric's early exit from the party. Or at least from kissing her.

She normally had all her defenses in place, the bright, bubbly slight ditzy Rachel that dated the wrong men and smiled at everyone.

But one minute with Danny and abruptly she'd lost her ability to fake social graces with a man? At this point she was probably expected to thank the big strong man for his presence; that is what a normal, whole, woman would do. Right? "Thank you," she added grudgingly, and then before she found herself saying anything else, she left.

"Rachel?"

Danny's voice had her stopping, and she pivoted to face him, temper spiking. If he was going to lecture her, tell her that she'd pretty much asked for Eric to turn into a handsy asshole, then she'd kill Danny dead. After taking Hope from him and putting her down somewhere safe, of course.

She'd heard the same shit before at college. He wouldn't say it outright; he'd maybe hint that her skirt was too short, or her top a little low cut, or maybe her lipstick was just a shade too red. She was used to that.

"What?" she asked, curtly, expecting the worst.

He held up his free hand in defense. "Woah, I was just going to say you don't need to thank me. I think you had it covered yourself. I was impressed."

Temper inside her eased from boiling to simmering. He near enough admitted right there and then that she didn't need a man sorting out her problems. She nodded once, and with determination carried on back into the party, schooling her features into happy-smiling-carefree Rachel. She was good at that.

Kyle swung her into a dance as soon as she stepped inside, hugging her close, then passing her to Cody, who had some serious moves. She danced opposite him, until she cried off saying she needed wine.

She spotted Danny at a corner table, rocking a car seat with Hope inside, and talking animatedly to Megan's mom. He looked up as she glanced over, and nodded to her. How had he known she was even looking?

And she had no idea what that nod meant. No idea at all.

She managed to get away from the dance floor, shimmied through the crowd to the open bar, grabbed two glasses of white wine, and went in search of Megan, who had positioned herself by the buffet table.

She immediately centered herself and ensured

she was smiling and that the smile reached her eyes. No point in Megan's night going downhill.

"Your boyfriend can sure move; I haven't seen that much hip action since... well ever."

Megan laughed. "You should see him in bed."

Rachel waved a hand to fan her face. "Don't start telling me sex stories now."

"I wasn't. Well, not much. So many stories so little time."

"Bitch," Rachel teased. She could do this. She could do *normal.*

"What happened with Eric?" Megan asked as she placed her wine down next to a plate of fresh fruit.

Rachel sipped hers, "He got handsy. I sent him home."

Megan sighed. "When are going to learn, he's just another idiot. Everyone knows he was a moron at school, and he's still one now."

"Yeah," Rachel said non-committedly. She wasn't ready for one of Megan's well-meaning talks about how Rachel was always going for losers; she'd heard them all before. Dating a loser as a defense mechanism worked well for her—no one expected too much, no one wanted too much.

Losers don't make you fall in love with them, lull you into a false sense of security, and then single-mindedly destroy you. She glanced over at Danny and met his steady gaze. He was staring at her, a thoughtful expression on his face, his head tilted a little to the left. She imagined he could see right through her, and that made her want to run. That was dangerous, and she didn't like treacherous and unpredictable.

She looked away and focused back on Megan.

"Why aren't you dancing?" She shimmied closer to her cousin and best friend.

"Because," Megan began patiently, "would you dance when you can stand here and get an eyeful of that? Not just one of them, but look, Danny's going up as well."

Rachel turned to see that Danny was moving to the dance floor, all sexy swagger, no sign of Hope in his arms, and then, like they'd planned it all, he slid easily into a complicated dance move with Cody, the two of them laughing like idiots.

Glancing back to where he'd been sitting, she saw that her aunt had Hope, still in the car seat, rocking her and staring down at the tiny baby.

Something indefinable snapped inside Rachel and grief too hard to handle filled her thoughts.

"See?" Megan said, her voice in the distance, her laughter loud. "That is what I want to watch, sexy men dancing."

But all Rachel wanted to do was run.

She nodded, and smiled, and talked to all the right people. She hugged her mom, kissed her dad, punched Kyle in the arm, and then she walked to the woman's restroom, an entire bottle of wine in her hand. She chose the last cubicle, locked the door, then sat on the closed lid, her feet up on the seat, her shoes on the floor, and the scent of a pine air freshener permeating her senses.

She drank the wine straight from the bottle, and let the grief and anger wash over her.

And she allowed herself to cry for everything she would never have.

And everything she'd always wanted.

Full time romance writer **Rozenn Scott** creates passionate love stories with a guaranteed happy ever after. Her series of novels, set in the beautiful Vermont town of Stanford Creek, focus on strong, independent women who find love.

Writing as RJ Scott, she is the author of over ninety bestselling gay romance novels and has never met a bottle of wine she can't defeat.

For more information on other books by RJ/Rozenn, visit her website: www.RJScott.co.uk.

CPSIA information can be obtained
at www.ICGtesting.com
Printed in the USA
BVOW06s1914261216
471852BV00001B/8/P